RUINED BEAUTY

ANGELS & BRUTES BOOK ONE

CARA BIANCHI

Copyright © 2023 - Cara Bianchi

Cover © 2023 - @covers_by_wonderland (Instagram)

All rights reserved.

No part of this book may be reproduced in any form or by any electronic or mechanical means, including information storage and retrieval systems, without written permission from the Author, except for the use of brief quotations in a book review.

AI Disclamer:

The Author expressly prohibits any platform from using this ebook in any manner for purposes of training artificial intelligence technologies to generate text. This includes, without limitation, technologies that are capable of generating works in the same style or genre as the Work. The Author reserves all rights to license uses of this ebook for generative AI training and development of machine learning language models.

No AI programs were used in the creation of this Work.

MAILING LIST

Join my mailing list and get a free spicy mafia romance novel in return. You'll also be the first to hear the latest Cara news!

Click here to join!

Connect with Me!

Follow me on Amazon here: Follow me

Find me on Instagram - @carabianchiwrites

Find me on TikTok - @carabianchiwrites

For the broken ones.

We fall hardest.

CONTENTS

Trigger warnings ix

Chapter 1	1
Chapter 2	5
Chapter 3	12
Chapter 4	17
Chapter 5	25
Chapter 6	32
Chapter 7	37
Chapter 8	43
Chapter 9	48
Chapter 10	53
Chapter 11	58
Chapter 12	64
Chapter 13	70
Chapter 14	75
Chapter 15	80
Chapter 16	85
Chapter 17	88
Chapter 18	93
Chapter 19	99
Chapter 20	104
Chapter 21	108
Chapter 22	113
Chapter 23	120
Chapter 24	128
Chapter 25	134
Chapter 26	139
Chapter 27	144
Chapter 28	151
Chapter 29	156
Chapter 30	164
Chapter 31	171

Chapter 32	178
Chapter 33	183
Chapter 34	186
Chapter 35	191
Chapter 36	197
Chapter 37	202
Chapter 38	206
Chapter 39	212
Chapter 40	220
Chapter 41	228
Chapter 42	232
Chapter 43	240
Chapter 44	247
Chapter 45	251
Chapter 46	255
Chapter 47	261
Chapter 48	267
Epilogue	273
Epilogue	282
Also by Cara Bianchi	291
Mailing List	293
Russian Phrases	295
Russian Patronymics	297

TRIGGER WARNINGS

I take your mental health seriously. I'm hesitant to label this book as dark or not, as it's highly subjective, but this book does contains material that may be distressing to some readers.

Graphic sexual content - the book is a slow-ish burn but the spice is spicy when it hits. Expect hand necklaces, masturbation, praise kink, come play, edging, spanking, anal play, and tons of very dirty talk indeed

Genre-typical violence - people die on the page. It's not gratuitous, but it's there, and includes use of guns, knives and a ligature

Alcohol use - on the page and frequent

Substance abuse - cocaine and heroin. Not depicted on the page but references made

Domestic violence - not depicted but referred to frequently

Mental health - panic attacks, PTSD, grief, depression

- **Abusive relationship dynamics** - control, possessiveness, coercion (there are no dub- or non-con elements to the sexual side of the story)

  Sexual violence/trafficking - references but nothing strong on the page

  Depiction of a character with a traumatic brain injury (TBI) - this is not meant to represent all (or any) real people who have a TBI. It's fiction and does not reflect an accurate or universal experience.

  Thanks for reading and proceed with caution if anything here might be difficult for you.

  If this is more of a shopping list than a warning, there's something wrong with you. And we should totally be friends.

1

Morgana

I take a few deep breaths, trying to slow my racing pulse. Hektor enjoys it too much when I'm nervous, and I want to keep a scrap of dignity.

Stay calm, Morgana. Get it together.

Hektor fancies himself as an intellectual, and meeting me at The Museum of Modern Art is his way of showing it. He doesn't know the difference between a Jackson Pollock and a puddle of vomit on the sidewalk.

Inside, the café is empty. Typical of Hektor to make them close the place just for him. He sits on the terrace in the sunshine, a couple of his favorite sycophants loitering nearby, and a guy named Bruno spots me.

"Hey, girl," he says, beckoning with his hand. "Come out here."

Hektor has the charmless smile of a man who doesn't have to play nice. "So, Morgana," he begins, leaning back in his chair. "My friend Vito called. He said you weren't good company last night."

I sit and put my rucksack on my knees, shielding myself. "I told you—I'm not willing to do... that. You told me I'd accompany rich old men to functions and laugh at their jokes."

"I've been more than patient with you." Hektor narrows his eyes. "You're not that naïve. Do you think you're so pretty that your precious face is worth paying for, and you can keep your pussy out of the transaction?"

I swallow, trying to suppress the tremble in my voice. "But he was so nasty. Everything was fine until I wouldn't go to his room, and then he tried to hit me. The hotel security had to intervene."

"I fucking know that," he snaps. "I threatened many people to get them to shut the fuck up. As for Vito, he's upset and embarrassed. You'd better believe me when I say it'll cost you."

Bruno's elbow seizes my neck. He hauls me to my feet, pressing the tip of a short dagger to my cheek.

"So what's it gonna be?" Hektor says. "Shall I have Bruno toss your frigid ass over the balcony, or should I be merciful and just carve your face? Honestly, I'm itching to pay your parents a visit. Bring your Mama on board. Some clients go for an older woman."

Panic throttles my voice. "Don't hurt her. I'll make it up to you. Just tell me what you want, and I'll do it!"

Hektor nods at Bruno, and he releases me, setting me on my feet.

"You are going out with Vito again tonight," Hektor says. "He has my permission to kill you if you try to refuse him. If you do what you're told, you join a new income bracket. Won't that be peachy?"

I nod. It's not as though I have a choice.

"Be ready to leave at seven p.m. I'll send a car." Hektor waves his hand at me. "Now get out of my fucking sight."

A minute later, I'm in the streets, surrounded by the good folks of the city. Living their everyday lives without a thought for how precarious it all is.

It's not the life I know. Not anymore.

My father is an accountant, and we had a lifestyle many would envy. It wasn't perfect; my mom was sick, but Dad and I cared for her.

We were doing just fine. Then Dad did something dumb.

He bought land to build and sell luxury condos, aiming to retire early and spend more time with Mom. But he had zero experience, and it was a con—the land was unsuitable. His finances deteriorated, and he and Mom were forced to sell our beautiful home and move us into a crappy two-bed apartment. I abandoned my photography course to be home with my mother during the day.

I'd never have met Hektor if I hadn't tried to help by taking a bar job. I still can't believe I was so gullible.

It's not even the first time. After what happened with Jack, I ought to have known better. Now Hektor has me in his clutches, and I have run out of chances. I fell so far, so fast.

I should hurry home. My mom's symptoms are flaring up. Dad can't pay for her meds, but after tonight, I'll have more money available, which is the slenderest of silver linings.

My backpack is slung over my shoulder, and my well-loved Panasonic compact camera is inside. I've hung onto it, although selling it would bring some much-needed income; Mom and Dad made me swear I would keep it. They know how much I love to find the story in a single image.

I head for the park, hoping it'll be quiet. Maybe I can find some beauty to capture before my life becomes uglier than I ever imagined.

2

Vlad

Papa is reading The Wall Street Journal. It makes him feel like a proper businessman rather than the white-collar criminal he is.

He glances at me but doesn't put the paper down. He'll give me his attention once he's good and ready.

Papa runs his eyes over me as I sit in the easy chair beside his bed. "You look like shit, Vladimir," he says, tossing the newspaper onto the floor.

That's rich coming from him. Does he think cancer of the lymph nodes makes him a pleasant sight?

I ignore his remark and reach for his water glass, holding the straw to his lips. He swats it away.

"If I wanted a nurse, I'd get a young one with big tits. I don't need *your* help."

Papa hates to be seen like this, with his mighty bulk atrophied away. The viciousness and hatred he spewed for years finally poisoned him, rotting his body before my eyes.

It's better than he deserves.

I'm his oldest son, but my father despises me. He cares about his children only when it comes to running his empire. Since my father's health declined, my Uncle David has been implementing Papa's decisions and keeping things going.

I have two brothers, and while Papa could theoretically name either of them as the next pakhan, it would be unwise. Avel is too young, and Sasha? No fucking way. I love the guy, but he's way too volatile. If we made him pakhan at eight a.m., we'd be at war before noon.

"What do you want, Papa?"

He rests bloodshot eyes on my face. "I need to put things in order. Are you ready to do your duty for me?"

Am I fuck. What I do, I'll do for me, and you will be in the cold ground where you can't mess with me anymore.

"Of course," I say. "Tell me what's gotta happen, and I'll see it done."

My father draws a rasping breath. "You will inherit control of all the legitimate businesses and associated accounts without checks or balances."

No shit. I've been running our companies for years. All *he* ever did was sign things.

"As for our Bratva interests, I need to know. Can you do it? Can you be a pakhan?"

"You know I can," I say, straining to keep my tone neutral. "How many people died at my hands to secure what's ours? All the billions of dollars I have laundered. The assets we legally own."

Papa's eyes are sunken and dull now, but I still see them in my nightmares. As a child, he would make me look at him while he beat me. It was supposed to make me tough enough to handle everything the bratva life would throw at me.

He couldn't hurt me now if his life depended on it. But I still fear that perhaps all that pain was for its own sake because he hated me then and hates me now.

When he summoned me to his bedside, he said he had a surprise for me. In all my forty-five years, a surprise from Papa has never been a good thing.

Fuck him.

"Oh, spit it out," I snarl. "I'm sick of you and your bullshit."

Papa sniffs. "Fine, you impudent prick. Here it is. You wanna be pakhan? Get married. Within the next week."

I wait for the punchline, but there's nothing except my father's wheezing breath. He unhooks the oxygen mask from the bedpost and places it over his mouth and nose, drawing deeply and keeping his eyes on mine.

"You fucking manipulative piece of—"

Papa removes the mask to yell. "I mean it, Vladi! The beneficiary codicil in my will cannot take effect unless I see you wed. And I will not formally name you as my successor in the bratva either. So you'd better make it look good for our associates too."

"Why?"

"It's tradition, of course." He sucks at his oxygen again for a few seconds before continuing. "Your grandfather cut me the same deal. It's meant to strengthen the incoming pakhan's claim because he's likely to produce an heir. And you're my oldest son and known to be highly competent, so it'd be strange if you didn't take over from me."

This is *not* what I want.

My parents' loveless arranged marriage ended a long-standing feud between the Kislevs and a prominent Italian mafia family. When I was born, Mama had someone to love, and Papa couldn't snuff out the joy I brought to her life. She and I had something he couldn't understand or take away, and he despised us both for it.

Mama bore him more children, and she loved us all, but Papa never hated them quite as much. Except for Lilyana, maybe.

I narrow my eyes. "What's the real reason you're doing this?"

"I know arranged marriages disgust you because you think I was cruel to your precious Mama." Papa meets my stony stare with one of his own. "Well, let me tell you this, boy. *I* didn't get to put my desires before duty, so neither will *you*. You wanna prove you're strong and focused enough to take the reins? Then do as I did. Take a wife you do not love, have children you do not want, and let your enemies know that Vladimir Kislev loves nothing but his bratva."

My father's speech has worn him out. Sweat beads on his brow, and he presses the mask to his face again, the clear plastic fogging as he tries to regain his breath.

So my destiny hinges on the capricious whims of a dying man.

"I enjoy playing God," Papa wheezes, as though he's reading my mind. "I should find Lilyana a brute of a husband and take her off your hands."

Threats to my little sister will tip me over the edge. If I don't get out of here, I will smother the bastard.

Papa's words follow me as I leave.

"It's on you, Vladi. Take a wife, or lose it all."

My office walls are closing in on me. Caffeine is calling, so I get an Americano with cream and take a walk.

I enter the park onto the path that runs close to the water's edge. It's relatively quiet, but I walk further than usual. I don't get enough solitude, and if I'm going to get my own coffee, I'll drink it in peace.

I round the corner to see a fight taking place.

Typical. I can't catch a break today.

A young woman struggles in a man's arms. He holds her waist, leaning back so she can't get much purchase on the ground. She kicks out in front of her, trying to fend off the attention of a second attacker holding a backpack.

"Get off me!" the woman cries. "Just take the bag and leave me alone!"

"I think I like you," the other man says, grabbing her flailing hand and putting it on his crotch. "Can you tell?"

There's nothing to think about. I move quickly, popping the lid of my cup and tossing the hot coffee straight into the man's leering face.

He screams and lets go of the woman's hand, and his companion shoves her toward me. She crashes into my chest, and I push her aside just in time to see a knife blade approaching me.

It's almost too easy to side-step and send the moron stumbling past me. A swift kick in the ass sees him fall head over foot down the embankment and into the pond, spluttering and cursing.

The other guy is coming back. I turn and flip open my jacket to ensure he sees my gun, holstered behind my right hip and tilted forward in the classic FBI style. Not that I'm FBI, of course. I have a mutually respectful relationship with law enforcement, so I don't hide that I'm armed. The coward backs away, then turns and runs, the woman's backpack still over his shoulder.

"Little shits," I say. "In broad daylight, too."

The young woman is sitting on the bench. She tilts her face to look at me, squinting in the light. The sight of her warms me more than the sun ever could.

Her hair is a rich auburn. It's wound on top of her head, unraveling slightly, loosened by the fight. Long feathery lashes frame her amber eyes, and her nose is sprinkled with freckles above her plump lips. A beauty spot high on her cheek accentuates her delicate bone structure.

I'm so distracted by her beauty that it takes a second for me to notice that she's in trouble. A rash-like flush is spreading across her chest and neck, and her jaw is working, her mouth opening and closing like a carp.

I drop to my knees in front of her and put my hands on her shoulders, propping her upright as she slumps.

"Breathe, *lisichka*. You're okay."

3

Morgana

I focus on the stranger's voice, my gasps deepening into steady breaths.

"Good girl." My rescuer stands and extends his hand, helping me to my feet.

Holy shit. Did he just *say* that?

He's at least fifteen years my senior and a foot taller, with the build of a man who has the time and money to take care of himself. Dark wavy hair, silvery at his temples. Shadow on his sharp jaw, deep slate-grey eyes.

I'm trying not to gawp, but he doesn't belong here on the streets like an average person. He looks like he fell off Mount Olympus and crash-landed in Hugo Boss.

"I'm sorry about that," I say. I glance past him at the pond. The guy he kicked in is nowhere to be seen. "I wanted to take photos, and those assholes got other ideas."

The stranger sits on the bench, patting the seat. "You need to take a minute."

I settle beside him, clasping my hands in my lap. My skirt seems too short, and I tug it over my bare thighs.

"Are you a photographer?"

"No," I say, embarrassed. "Not a professional. But I want to be a photojournalist. Interviews, human interest stories, that kind of thing."

He smiles. "You were planning on taking Pulitzer-prize-winning photos of what? The egrets?"

I can't tell if he's just teasing or being condescending. "No. I was just trying to shake off an awful morning."

"It's only ten a.m.," he laughs. "Are things that bad already?"

A rush of nausea hits. The adrenaline is wearing off, and this day will get far worse. A few minutes of conversation with a hot stranger won't change that.

"Nothing to see here," I say with a sigh. "A day in the life of me."

"And who's you?"

"Morgana Bloom." We shake hands. "Twenty-seven, failed journalist, all-round incompetent human being. And you?"

"Vladimir Kislev. But you can call me Vlad."

His hand is large and warm. He holds on longer than appropriate, and I pull my hand back, avoiding his eyes.

"I'd better go."

"Why? You have an interview with someone other than a wading bird?"

I shrug. "No, I don't. Now I don't even have a camera. So it's all going well."

"I'll replace your camera, so you can interview *me*."

Is he famous? He's so sexy. It seems impossible he *isn't* a celebrity.

"Are you somebody I should recognize? I'm not good at names."

"That's a handicap for a world-class interviewer."

"I'm not a world-class *anything*."

"Everyone has to start somewhere." He smiles at my baffled frown. "It's no big deal, but I'm a billionaire." He sets off back along the path to the park entrance. "Walk with me."

I scurry behind him. "You are? But I don't have my stuff. No camera, no Dictaphone, nothing."

"I'll give you a ride home, and we'll make a date." Vlad stops beside an ice cream cart. "Two, please. Dulce de leche."

"It's okay. I won't have one."

He shakes his head, handing me a cone. "You're a journalist —you can't turn down a scoop. And this one is perfect. Cold, sweet, rich, *and* kinda sexy. You don't look like a vanilla girl to me."

A ghost of a smile, a twinkle in his eye. There's no denying it. This gorgeous man is flirting with me.

I take the cone. "Are you still talking about the ice cream?"

"That sounds like a question, Miss Bloom." He arches an eyebrow, and I melt a little. "If you're gonna interview me, you gotta do it right. You'll need pictures of me in my home to set the right tone. And I'll pay you, of course."

My phone is ringing, and I take it from my pocket, glad of the diversion. Before I can look at the screen, Vlad snatches it from my hand.

"I want your full attention, Morgana." He swipes to red, hanging up the call. "You have *mine*, so it's only fair."

Goddammit! Who the *fuck* does he think he is?

"Give me that back! You can't do whatever you want."

"What kind of gratitude is that?" He holds my phone above his head. "I just saved you *and* lost my coffee."

I snatch at his hand, but it's hopeless. He smirks, and I glower at him.

"I said I'd pay you for your company," he grins. "Would that be so bad?"

Men think *everything* can be bought.

I cannot believe I'm dealing with this from a stranger. I expected it from Hektor, but this guy? He doesn't even *know* me.

"I appreciate what you did," I seethe, "but I'm *not* for sale."

Vlad laughs as he hands back my phone. "*Lisichka*, everything is for sale, especially when *I'm* buying. It's cute that you think you can say no to me."

That is *it*.

Anger boils over. My arm darts out, and before he can stop me, I smoosh the ice cream into Vlad's silk jacket. He looks at his chest with a frown as I rummage in my pocket.

"That's for the coffee," I hiss, tossing a ten-dollar bill in his face, "and you can keep your fucking scoop."

I turn and walk away, breathing deeply to calm my shredded nerves. I'm still rattled from the attack, or I *think* that's what it is. But maybe it was that beautiful man who set my pulse racing again.

I know I'm overreacting. My head was a mess already before Vlad rescued me—he didn't deserve to get covered in caramel gelato. The suit I ruined was probably worth five times my rent arrears.

He was arrogant and stomped all over my boundaries, making me furious, yet aroused. He didn't know what his presence was doing to me, so I must have looked pretty crazy when I chewed him out and stormed off.

What a dumb thing to do. If he really was gonna pay me to interview him, it's a damn sight better than lying on my back under some other wealthy asshole.

I turn around, but Vlad is nowhere to be seen.

Something about him pulls at me. Who *is* he, though? *Kislev.* It sounds familiar, but we definitely haven't met before. God knows I'd have remembered him.

4

Morgana

The hours passed all too quickly, and now it's almost time.

Sex for money. The oldest profession. I never dreamed I'd experience this level of dehumanization, but at least I'll enjoy a taste of the high life.

Who am I kidding? I don't look down on sex workers; people do what they gotta do. But I never thought I'd become one.

The green satin dress is too short. It's from Hektor's collection, to ensure I look as expensive as his fees suggest.

My phone rings. I glance at the screen to see it's my friend Josie, and I swipe to green, putting the phone on speaker.

"Hi, Morgana," she says. "News got around. Apparently, you're giving a client the full package?"

Josie works for Hektor, too, and is more at peace with it than I am, but Hektor would kill her if she tried to run away. When we met, she warned me he would turn on me eventually. I didn't listen, but we became firm friends, and although she's a little younger than me, she's far more worldly.

"I have zero options," I say. "If I don't do whatever Vito tells me, Hektor will turn my parents and me into modern art."

"I'm sorry, but it was always gonna come to this. Just get Vito off quickly, then bail. Or pretend to love it. Ever seen Pretty Woman?"

I accidentally smudge a blob of mascara onto my nose. "Yes, I have. It's a movie. Life doesn't work that way. And I don't want to be a kept woman."

"Be honest—if it were Richard Gere, it'd be awesome."

"Funny you should say that because I met a billionaire today." I line my eyes with a kohl pencil. "He offered to let me interview him."

"Sounds good. Is he hot?"

Oh fuck, yes.

"I didn't notice. And I walked away without getting his number, so it won't happen anyway."

I know Josie too well. She's about to grant me her penetrating insight, whether or not I wanna hear it.

"You've put your dreams on hold and ended up in the gutter because of your father's mistakes," she says. "But don't write yourself off *yet*, honey."

"My dreams are *dead*, not on hold," I say, applying rose-pink lipstick. "I'm trapped. And my father means well, even if he goes about it all wrong. Mom needs him so much. She's frail these days and can't handle the stress."

"Her Addison's symptoms still bad?"

"Yes." I blink away tears, trying to stop my eyeliner from running. "I took her some soup earlier, but she's been asleep otherwise. I'll get her pills when I can afford them. But I can't let my parents discover how much trouble I've gotten into. It'd kill them."

Josie hears the wobble in my voice and changes tack. "Come on. Tell me more about your billionaire."

"He's not *my* billionaire. And I'm about to become a fully-fledged call girl. I have bigger problems than some rich hottie."

"There are good men out there, Morgana. You might meet one someday."

"I don't *want* to fall in love again. It sucked last time." I scowl at myself in the mirror. "I'm defective, and it must show. How else do these evil bastards find me? It's not as though I take out ads that say, 'Naive damaged goods seeks abusive asshole. Must be willing to raise hopes of happiness only to dash to the ground. No timewasters.'"

"Hey, don't be that way," she says, her voice soothing. "And as for the job, it's not that bad. Clients are wealthy too. If one takes a shine to you, he'll pay your bills and spoil you. And if you don't expect love or affection, that's as good as it gets."

"I guess."

"Remember—get through the first time, and it'll never be this bad again."

A car engine outside.

"Gotta go."

I glance out of the window. A white Mercedes S-class sedan is pulling up in the lot.

Here I go.

My heart is in my mouth as I make my way downstairs.

Through the frosted glass of the main door, I see a shadow. Dad is there, talking to someone.

It's been months since he was home before nine p.m. on a Friday. What am I gonna tell him? I have nowhere to hide, and the car is waiting for me. Obviously, I don't work in a bar, not dressed like this.

There's nothing for it. I swallow hard and fling the door open.

Vladimir Kislev is standing there. I glance from him to my father and back again.

You have to be fucking kidding me.

"I don't understand," my father says, addressing Vlad. "You've cleared my debt?"

"Every cent, George."

Dad does not allow strangers to call him by his first name. He's Mr. Bloom, and he *insists* on it. But Vlad just called him

George, and I'm astonished to hear no admonishments from my father's lips, no demands for respect.

"What the hell is this meant to be?" Dad asks, gesturing at my clothes.

"I... I have a date."

"The fuck you do," Vlad snaps.

I ignore him. "What's he talking about, Dad? What debt?"

"Allow me," Vlad says. He palms his wavy hair, sweeping it back from his forehead, and fixes his smoky eyes on mine. "After you ran out on me today, I looked you up. Your father owed five million dollars to a friend of mine, and even after your dear Papa gave him every scrap of money he could find, he was still two million short of clearing the debt. So I cleared it for him."

The money my father borrowed was dirty? It makes perfect sense. I can't believe I didn't figure it out.

"That means your father now owes *me*." Vlad raises an eyebrow. "And he has something I want."

"You can't do this," Dad interjects. "Morgana is my daughter. I love her. Can't you understand that?"

"I don't fucking care." My father shrinks away as Vlad takes a step toward him. "You think you have things to worry about? Fuck me around and see what happens. Your daughter belongs to *me*, and *you* get to live another day. Simple."

The pain on my father's face is more than I can bear, and I hurl myself at Vlad, clawing for his eyes. He ducks under my flailing arms and throws me over his shoulder, ignoring me as I beat my fists on his back.

"Put me down, you sick asshole!"

"Has that ever worked?" Vlad asks. "Why even say it?"

Did you think I'd thank you and let you take Morgana in return?" my father asks, his voice rising in panic. "What is *wrong* with you?"

Vlad doesn't react to my wriggling. His arm is rock solid around my waist, his other hand on the back of my thigh.

"I expected more gratitude," he says. "And as for what's wrong with me, we'd be here forever. But I'll make it easier for you. I *am* taking your daughter. And if she refuses, I'll murder you right here." He swats my ass with his palm. "You hear that, *lisichka*? If you want to watch your father bleed out, all you have to do is carry on just as you're doing now."

I stop fighting and stay still, my arms hanging down Vlad's back. Something in his tone is terrifyingly casual, and I don't think he's joking.

I can't see my father, but I hear him. I've never known him to stutter before.

"N-n-no. You c-can't—"

"It's okay, Dad," I say. "Let me go."

Vlad turns and sets off toward his car. I wave my hand at my father.

"Look after Mom. She needs you. I'll be fine."

Vlad laughs, and I can't help myself. I raise my knee sharply, digging him in the ribs, and he responds by grasping my thigh and squeezing hard.

"Do that again, and I'll tie you up and put you in the trunk. Right before I go back and kill your father for raising such a brat."

He sets me on my feet, leaning to open the passenger door, and I catch his scent. Something expensive. Cedar, tobacco, cardamom.

"You don't understand." He pushes me into the seat. "Hektor will kill us all when he finds out what you've done!"

Vlad slams the car door, cutting me off mid-panic, and climbs into the driver's seat beside me. The engine roars to life.

"*You* don't understand, Morgana." His eyes flash over my body briefly before returning to my face. "I didn't pay two million dollars to have you for one night. You're gonna marry me."

I stare at him as he turns the car around.

He's out of his damn mind.

"What the hell makes you think I'll agree to *that*?"

"It's like I said—everything's for sale. You're bought and paid for. It's all above board."

"Except for the part where you threatened to kill my father?"

He shrugs. "The carrot-and-stick theory is solid. Money is the carrot, but that doesn't mean I won't wield huge fuck-off sticks when required. In my world, that's how deals are done."

"What world is that?"

"The bratva. The Russian mob. Get used to it." Vlad pulls up at the junction out of the parking lot. "Which way?"

"I don't know what you—"

Vlad glances at me, his expression stony. "Which way to Hektor?"

"You can't just—"

"Morgana," he says, his voice firm. "Tell me *now*."

"He has a bolt-hole in Yorkville."

5

Vlad

Morgana's red hair falls in smooth waves over her shoulder. She looks beautiful, but her getting dolled up for another man makes me want to find the fucker and pull his eyes from their sockets.

She bowled me over when she left me soaked in ice cream and her rage. No woman ever talked to me like that, and I loved it. I had to know about the enchanting girl with a Pre-Raphaelite face, slightly slutty clothes, and soulful eyes. What was her deal?

I gave her name to Arman, and he went to work. My adopted brother is excellent at tracking people down, and when he came to me a couple of hours ago and told me who Morgana was, I laughed my ass off.

My family built our fortune on the backs of idiots like George Bloom. Optimists don't realize that a leap of faith can break your back if you land too hard.

It was simple to buy George's debt and therefore own him *and* his pretty daughter. He was heartbroken to lose Morgana in such a sordid way, but it's not my fault he's dumb enough to borrow from the underworld.

Of course, I could have taken Morgana *without* doing her father a favor, but he's a civilian, so it's frowned upon. Besides, I'm asking a lot of her, and it might be less of a bind if she can console herself knowing that her parents' financial problems are over.

But Arman never mentioned a boyfriend.

"So, who is this Hektor?"

Morgana sniffs, and I realize she's crying. She's trying to hide it by turning her face to the window, but I hear it in her voice.

"He's a pimp, alright?" she snaps. "Not a boyfriend or anything, not anymore. I was meant to go out with a client."

"So I assume you never took him home to meet your folks?"

"They don't know about it. I was trying to help and got in too deep. And now Bruno will arrive at seven to collect me, find I'm not there, and then fuck knows what'll happen. It's gonna be difficult for you to threaten my parents' lives if someone else kills them, right?"

Yes. But that's not my primary concern.

I glance at my watch. "It's six-fifteen now. We'll be in Yorkville in ten minutes, so I'll have this dealt with by... six forty-five?"

I keep my eyes on the road, but I feel Morgana staring at me.

"What are you gonna do? Hektor isn't from New York. He probably doesn't know who you are."

Which means his friends are not my friends. Not well-connected and therefore didn't ring the cherries when Arman asked around.

"Threats to you are threats to me, and I'm not gonna tolerate that from anyone, least of all some gang-banging scumbag. You belong to *me* now, and that's all there is to it." I put my foot down, gaining speed. "He'll know who I am before the hour is out, *lisichka*. Mark my words."

∽

Along an alley, a burly man stands at the door of a dive bar.

"That's Bruno," Morgana says.

I exit the car, catching Bruno's eye as I walk to the passenger side. He frowns as I open the door.

"You stay with me." I grip Morgana's hand. "I'd rather get you to safety, but there's no time, and I can't leave you in the car."

"Don't." She tries to take back her hand, but I have too tight a hold. "Please. I'm so scared. I can't take all this in. It's happening too fast."

"You're mine," I say, pulling her with me. "I don't intend to give any of these fuckers a chance to argue otherwise. Stay with me and do what I say, no matter what. You understand?"

She nods, stumbling a little on her high heels. Bruno steps forward to meet me, squaring his chest, and points at Morgana.

"*That* does not belong to you. Who the *fuck* do you think—"

I let go of Morgana and land a solid left hook on Bruno's jaw. Blood flies as he crashes into the dumpster, hitting his head hard. I stoop to Bruno and punch him in the solar plexus, knocking the breath from him. He heaves and falls on his side.

They're all the same, these guys. Big, but slow. I'm pretty stacked too, but the difference is that I act decisively and don't second-guess myself. I'd rather fuck someone up too much than too little.

I pull my gun from the holster.

Morgana screams.

I turn and look at her. "You're really not getting it, are you?"

"You can't just shoot people in the fucking street!" she cries.

Bruno crawls to the other side of the dumpster, and I follow him.

"Oh my God, Vlad! Don't—"

I ignore Morgana's protests and shoot Bruno in the back of the head. He slumps onto the concrete, blood pooling beneath him. Morgana appears beside me and gasps.

"Jesus Christ! You blew him away just like that? You didn't even speak to him!"

I take her hand again. "I had nothing to say. You need to get used to this. It's your life now."

The bar is deserted. The dull thump of a bass speaker shakes the ceiling. What sort of dimwit posts a guard on the door but then plays his music too loud to hear what's happening? I thought I might be underestimating the guy, but I don't think that's possible.

We head upstairs, and Morgana nods at a door. "In there. But his girls will be here, his junkie friends, who knows? You'll be outnumbered."

"It won't matter."

I put my gun away and rap my knuckles on the door. A rail-thin girl opens it a couple of inches on the chain. She has a yellowish bruise on her cheekbone.

"I'm here to speak to Hektor. About Morgana."

The girl turns away. "It's a man wanting to talk to Hektor. He has a red-haired girl with him. He says her name is Morgana?"

"Did Bruno collect that slut already?" a voice shouts, and someone turns the music down. "For fuck's sake. I told him to get someone to take his guard post! Let him in."

It's a studio apartment. A handful of sick-looking girls line the walls, passing blunts and crack pipes around. In the middle, three men sit on a corner couch, their boots on the coffee table. I see a dusty-looking mirror and some razor blades beside them.

Cokeheads spend as much money as they make. Only undisciplined losers get into that shit, which figures. Do these fuckers think they can come to New York City and start their own little vice kingdom without paying dues?

"Which one of you is Hektor?" I say.

The man in the middle frowns. He's younger than me, but he's been in the wars. A ragged scar rings his neck—

someone clearly tried to do the world a favor and slit his throat. Well, his luck just ran out.

"What's it to you?" Hektor asks, getting to his feet. "And what the *fuck*," he spits, jabbing his finger at Morgana, "are *you* playing at? Didn't I make myself clear this morning? Where is Bruno?"

"Dead behind the dumpster outside," I say. "Go take a look."

Hektor moves to the window, looking into the street below.

"Oh shit," one of the goons says. "Hektor, don't fuck with him. That's Vladimir—"

I throw Morgana behind me and draw my pistol, shooting Hektor neatly through his eye. He sways and falls, but I'm already firing at one of his goons as he stands. He takes two in the chest and spins, falling face-first into the coffee table and smashing it to smithereens.

The junkie girls are whimpering on the floor. I saw the third guy in my peripheral—he's now low on the other side of the couch, so I duck and shift alongside it.

Morgana is on the ground, lying on her front. She catches my eye, her expression glacial.

Fuck me. This woman hates my guts. Papa will be delighted.

I press my pistol to the back of the couch.

"Do you wanna live, *tovarishch*?" I shout.

"*Da*," a voice replies. "*Da*, Vladimir Sergeyevich Kislev, *sdavat'sya*. I surrender."

I pinpoint his location from his voice and adjust my aim. The bullet passes through the couch and pierces the man's throat. He gurgles as he collapses beside his dead friend, and I administer the coup de grâce with the last bullet in the chamber.

Apart from the girls' sobs, all is quiet. Morgana glares at me as she sits up.

"You need to let these girls go."

"Fine." I holster my weapon and reach for my wallet. Morgana's eyes widen as I hand her a thick sheaf of bills. "Share this out amongst them. I'll keep watch and shift Bruno into the dumpster."

6

Morgana

I send the girls out with full pockets. Some may make it out of this life, but most will smoke and snort the money away and be back at square one.

Bruno's body has gone, but I don't look inside the dumpster. I don't need to see that again.

Vlad is beside the car, pacing as he talks on the phone. He looks like any successful guy dealing with business. But he's also a person who can kill four men without showing the slightest sign that it bothers him. As I draw nearer, he raises his voice, bellowing into his cell.

"Sasha, *bratan*, just deal with it. I don't want *dyadya* David involved. He gets in his head about this stuff, as though I need to complete forms in triplicate before I can murder someone. I'll be in charge soon, so you should get used to doing what you're fucking told."

He gives me a lop-sided grin and opens the passenger door for me. "I'll tell you why later," he says into the phone. "Right now, I want it done. *Poymi menya*?" He points at the seat and presses his phone to his chest, covering the speaker. "Get in, *lisichka*. We're going home."

I sit in the car and watch Vlad finish his phone call.

His nonchalance chills me. When he bought my father's debt, he honestly believed he'd bought me too, like there was no other interpretation, and fell back on threats when my father said otherwise.

I had to go with him, or my family would die. I had nothing to negotiate with and no incentive to make him reconsider. He decided he wanted *me*, and that was it. What was there to discuss?

I'm a magnet for toxic men. Always have been. With a sick mother and a workaholic father, I was a latchkey kid, starved for companionship and attention.

It's no wonder I fell for Jack. He wanted to be at my side every minute, and I ate it up. I swore I'd never fall for that spiel again, but when Hektor came along, I thought he was different.

Now Vlad. This is the man I met just hours ago when I was in danger, and he saved me. Now he's done it again, but it hits differently this time.

My first impressions let me down again. At least I'm going into this with my eyes open.

He's just a bad guy. Nothing else to see.

~

We park on Riverside Drive, and my jaw drops.

The property is on the corner, rounded like a tower. It sticks out like aliens beamed up a chunk of a castle and dumped it there.

"This is your house?"

Vlad is unphased. "I'm a billionaire, Morgana. This place will be mine, and it will be yours, too. But you gotta play your part."

His gray eyes seize mine, and I can't look away. He doesn't speak, and the atmosphere is suddenly thick with tension.

"Let me make my expectations perfectly clear," Vlad begins. "I need a wife, and you are gonna take that role. I'm not stupid enough to kill your parents at your first sign of resistance, but I will take them captive if you force my hand. Believe me when I say I'm absolutely fucking serious."

He murdered four people in front of me. Does he think I doubt him *now*?

"You need to play along," he says. "It has to look real."

"You threaten my family and steal me away, and you think I can pretend to be in love with you? What kind of Oscar-winning actor do you think I am?"

He grins. "You're fun, Morgana. Most women I meet are just cardboard cutouts. They clamor for my attention or, if they're bratva, they've been raised to have no interests or personality. When we met this morning, you took a liking to me. Since then, I've probably ruined that impression, but you can channel it into your performance."

Ruined Beauty

I want to tell him to fuck himself, but his lips curl, and I have to concede that he's correct. I *did* like him. In fact, I couldn't stop thinking about him.

But Vlad's life is a million times removed from mine. If someone had told me I'd be his fiancé before the day was through, I'd have said they needed their head examined. Does he think *everyone* is so shallow that money can paper over the cracks?

My father made so many mistakes. He wanted to secure our future but lost everything. His life was all he had left; from what Vlad said, he would have lost that too. How could that be worth it?

He got desperate. I can't make him suffer even more just because he did the wrong thing for the right reasons.

Vlad couldn't understand that in a million years. He just swept in and took advantage.

"Why are you doing this, anyway?" I ask him. "You must have women falling over themselves to get next to you. Are you such a bastard that your looks don't compensate for your personality?"

I gave myself away a bit there. What is *wrong* with me?

Vlad sits back a little, giving me a better view of his broad chest. His shirt is unbuttoned just enough at the neckline for me to see his collarbone, and despite the situation, I'm struck by the image of running my tongue over it.

"Thanks very much, *lisichka*. And since you asked, the issue is time-sensitive. Part of the Russian tradition of," he affects a stronger accent, "*notya*."

"And that means...?"

"It means notya concern. So keep your pretty little nose out." He grins at my irritation. "Relax. You'll be Morgana Georgevna Kisleva before the week is out. The advantages will make up for my character defects, I promise."

7

Morgana

Inside, the house is like nothing I've ever seen.

We enter a foyer with a polished wood floor and a red-carpeted staircase. Silk Damask furniture lines a viewing area that leads into a snug den, just visible through the half-open sliding doors. To the right is a grand piano, as shiny as obsidian.

"Do you play?"

Vlad shakes his head. "It belongs to my sister." He leads me upstairs. "There's an elevator," he says, "but I'd better walk you through the house at least once."

Each room is more sumptuous than the last. Nooks and dens and bedrooms and bathrooms. A library. A theater. Several studies. The roof terrace is large enough to seat a hundred people, and Vlad tells me that's where we'll hold our wedding reception.

"How many bedrooms?"

"Eight. My father lives on the fifth floor with my uncle, and the rest of my family has rooms too. The third floor is for us."

"So, who am I gonna meet?"

Vlad stops outside a door. "I have two brothers and a sister, all younger than me. My father also adopted the son of a murdered ally, so he's practically family now." He lowers his voice. "My father is sick. He wants this marriage to happen, so there's no time to waste. You'd better act crazy about me and be thrilled to become my wife. That's what I expect and what you'll give me. Understood?"

I've never wished more fervently for superpowers. What I wouldn't give to set this asshole on fire with my eyes.

"Whatever," I say, giving him the bitchiest glare I can muster.

Vlad pushes open the door. Three men stand, but one does not.

A pale, thin old man sits on a chaise longue, an IV bag on a stand beside him. A tube is attached to his arm with a cannula.

"Ah, so this is my daughter-in-law!" he says as we enter. "*Dobryy vecher*, sweet girl. I am Sergey Kislev."

"Papa," Vlad says, his tone sharp. "This is Morgana."

I take Sergey's hand. It's cold and slightly moist, his grip almost non-existent.

"I'm pleased to meet you." I try to keep my voice light. "You have a beautiful home."

"I know."

Sergey smiles, showing his small yellowing teeth. His contempt for Vlad and me is apparent, and he does not try to hide it.

"Don't be smug, Papa," another man says, approaching me. "It's not as though you chose any of the fittings."

He takes my hand and shakes it firmly. He's not as tall as Vlad but just as muscular, his shoulders and arms straining the fabric of his black t-shirt. His eyes are bluer than Vlad's, and as he grins broadly at me, I'm surprised to see a ring through his lip. His dark hair is long enough on top to be tied in a scruffy knot, but the sides are shaved short, complimenting his neat beard. Apart from his face, every inch of visible skin is covered in tattoos.

So this is the bad boy of the family.

"I'm Alexandr, but no one calls me that, so I wouldn't think to answer to it. You can call me Sasha."

"Thanks, I will." I smile at him, and Vlad takes my hand, squeezing it hard.

Is he jealous? *Jesus.* I'm saying hello. Should I spit in his brother's eye just to make a point?

And this," Sasha gestures to the young man behind him, "is Avel. You don't have to show him any respect, don't worry." He turns around. "What are you now? Twelve?"

Avel scowls. He looks like a younger Vlad, but he's not twelve. I'd say more like eighteen. Sharp cheekbones and a sculpted jaw, with hair just long enough to shade his pale grey eyes. This kid looks like he could bully a girl to tears, and she'd still be crushing on him.

I look past Sasha and wave at Avel. "Hi."

Avel waves back. He has the studied sneer of the arrogant youth, and I like him for it. Teenagers are teenagers, even in the bratva.

"Ignore him," Vlad says. "He's a moody prick, but we all had our moments when we were his age, so apart from the occasional slap round the head, we leave him be. Don't we, *mladshiy brat*?"

Avel flips him off, and I choke back laughter.

"Cheeky little shit," Vlad says.

He leads me to the only remaining stranger in the room, a lean guy with a grown-out buzz cut and neatly trimmed stubble. He's dressed in black, with a thin gold chain at his neck, and his eyes are as dark as the rest of him.

"This intense-looking motherfucker is Arman." Vlad slaps him on the shoulder. "His father was murdered, thanks to *my* father's inattention to detail—"

"Fucking watch your mouth, Vladi," Sergey says.

Vlad ignores him and continues. "—so he's now a member of this family. He's lived and worked with us for many years."

Arman doesn't smile, and I'm glad to let go of his hand. "Didn't you mention a sister, too?" I ask. "And your uncle?"

"David is out attending to some business," Sergey says. "Lilyana does not join the family in the evenings, but you will meet her eventually."

Tension is coming off Vlad in waves. *Shit.* This is all so dreamlike that I'd forgotten the grim reality. He told me to make it look good, so I'd better try.

"So I can't wait to marry Vladi," I trill, taking Vlad's arm. "When I met him, I never thought he'd be interested in me, but I guess I really lucked out!"

The silence is crippling. Sergey raises his eyebrows at me.

"Lucky, lucky girl. True love found you. How *special*."

It strikes me that a game is being played, and I'm just one piece on the board, being moved around at the players' whims but with no knowledge of the bigger picture.

I want to get out of here.

"Didn't you tell me there's a terrace?" I grasp Vlad's hand. "Show me the view over the Palisades."

"You got it." Vlad nods at his father. "Morgana and I will move into the third floor, and tomorrow I'll get everything she needs for the wedding. Don't bring me any business until that's dealt with. Have a good evening, everyone."

Vlad's hand is on the door handle when Sergey speaks.

"Give her a kiss, Vladi."

Sergey sits perfectly still, his cold eyes fixed on Vlad. His sons are all staring at him, but no one says anything.

"I want to see the love you have for one another." Sergey clasps his hands together in his lap. "It's a wonderful thing. Humor an old man, won't you?"

Vlad squeezes my hand hard enough to hurt, and I bite my lip.

"I'm kidding." Sergey laughs. "Lighten up, boy."

Vlad says nothing. As we leave, he slams the door behind us.

8

Vlad

The view from the terrace never changes. Sitting here, the lights reflecting in the river—it could be a romantic moment. But it isn't.

"You've stolen me." Morgana's tone is listless. "That's all there is to it. My parents are safe. No money trouble, no creditors looking for them. But my life isn't my own."

"That was true *before* I showed up," I say, topping off her glass of prosecco. "The bratva world isn't all bad. You'll have every luxury you ever dreamed of."

She confuses me. I didn't expect her to be delighted to marry me, and getting to know me won't make her any more amenable, but I thought my wealth might placate her.

I sip my vodka. "You were on the verge of whoring yourself out. Your father had no more money, and he'd have been murdered for sure. None of that is a problem now. I clicked my fingers, and it was gone."

"The same goes for people, right?" she asks. "It was kinda impressive, but I didn't want to witness those men being murdered, however much I hated them. I don't want your life. I want *mine*."

"Okay, look. I have to get married to inherit the bratva and the money after my father's death. Once that's done, I don't give a shit if he croaks before the ink is dry. When he's gone, and everything is mine, you can leave and do whatever the fuck you like. But you'll remain under my protection, and I'll give you ten million dollars a year by way of thanks."

Morgana says nothing for a moment. I expected a reaction; most find that kind of money impressive.

"I need to ask you something." Her voice quivers. "Am I expected to sleep with you? Is that part of the deal?"

Her fear shames me. I *could* insist on fucking her—she has no power here. But I don't want to force her. My father did that to my mother, and it broke something in her soul.

I knock back my drink. "To be honest, I'd be delighted to fuck you, but I won't *make* you sleep with me. I don't want a wife who despises me more than necessary. It's dangerous. So we can keep sex out of it if you prefer, but as far as anyone else is concerned, we're screwing each other's brains out."

Morgana's eyes move over my body, and I detect a crumb of ambivalence.

"Unless you want to add some terms and conditions of your own, *lisichka*?"

"No." She looks away, but I see her blush. "I want my parents to survive and to get away from you. It's in my interests to cooperate with this insane charade."

"So we agree on something." I stand and reach for her. "Come on. I'll show you our suite."

~

"The entire floor is for you?" Morgana gasps as we exit the elevator.

"Learn not to show it if you're impressed by luxury," I say, "or you'll embarrass me in public. This floor used to belong to Mama. After she died, my father used to have parties up here and trash it, but since he got sick, all that stopped. I ordered a full refurbishment at the first opportunity."

We head into the bedroom, and I point at a second door. "That leads to our lounge and, beyond that, the dressing room. The ensuite has a walkthrough rainforest shower and a bathtub. My mother brought it from a Venetian palace, and it was her pride and joy."

Morgana touches the marble mantlepiece but avoids looking at the king-size bed. "So this is how criminal royalty lives."

The women who move in my circle are jaded. They don't care about themselves or the trappings of the lifestyle. But Morgana's desires can't be bought, and although she's unfamiliar with what real money can buy, I don't think she will ever become one of the superficial dolls that are commonplace in my world. She has ambitions, just like me, but she abandoned them to ensure the safety of those she cared about.

Something becomes clear as she runs her fingertips along the velvet drapes.

I can force her to marry me, keep her captive in luxury, and fuck her day and night if I choose, but I can't make her *care*. Not about me.

"The kitchen is downstairs," I say. "Use the intercom by the elevator to call and ask for anything you like. The closet is stocked for you, but not everything will fit. Tomorrow you can do some shopping. You'll need a wedding dress."

"I need to call my friend and tell her what's happening. She works for Hektor too—shit!" Morgana spins to face me, her eyes wild. "Hektor's client will wonder where I am by now. There's no one to even take his calls."

"Hookers aren't hard to find. Tell your friend to meet you for a wedding boutique appointment tomorrow morning."

Morgana opens her mouth to say something, but nothing comes out.

"I need to speak to my uncle," I say. "Stay here and explore the suite, and I'll get us some food. Anything you especially like?"

"I'd kill for a burger." She frowns at my laughter. "Why is that funny?"

"I'm sorry. I don't know any women who eat. Most just pick at nothing. If you want a burger, that's what I'll get for you. I'm partial to them myself." I remember what I needed to ask her. "Who was your client, by the way?"

Morgana cocks her head. "A guy called Vito Serra. He's horrible. I went to dinner with him last night, and he tried to hit me."

I turn away fast so she doesn't see the rage on my face.

That's enough for me. The fucker is *dead*.

Despite my efforts to hide it, Morgana picks up on my fury. "Oh no," she says, taking a step toward me. "From what he told me, he's not some two-bit loser like Hektor. Don't go looking for him. You'll get hurt."

I look at her, furrowing my brow. "The fuck do you care?"

"I don't, but you might get murdered. What will happen to *me* then?"

My uncle David would continue to care for the bratva's interests. Still, Morgana would either be eliminated before she became a liability or gifted to a rival to sweeten a deal.

"I'm not going anywhere tonight, *lisichka*." I make for the door. "Call your friend."

9

Vlad

"*Dyadya*, I need a word."

David hangs up his coat. "I'm sure you do. You left a pile of corpses in some Yorkville shithole, correct?"

How the fuck does he know that?

David sees the question on my face. "I was at Joe Morelli's café, talking a little business. One of his busboys said he'd seen you going into a bar with a girl."

"That doesn't tell you shit," I say. "You went looking for me?"

"I was curious, so I stuck my head through the door. Were you gonna just leave a mess?"

I hate his nagging tone. Doesn't he realize he'll be answering to me soon?

David is more intelligent than my father but cut from the same cloth. Like me, he's the less-favored son, but he's the younger of the two and never married. It's as though protecting and serving the family is David's way of honoring his father, despite their distant relationship. I can relate to that, but Papa has recently given him a little responsibility, and he's gotten too used to it.

"Sasha wrangled a clean-up crew," I say. "Should the Pakhan-in-waiting be on his knees picking up bits of skull? We pay people to do that."

"It's not good business to kill people first and ask questions later," David says, following me into the rear lounge.

"Maybe not," I say, "but the guy didn't show respect. If he'd had the sense to come to us, we'd have appraised him of the fucking rules. His lack of manners got him killed."

David goes to the drinks trolley and pours himself a vodka. He doesn't offer me one.

"Did it occur to you," he says, sitting on a leather armchair, "that he might be under someone's protection? He worked for a rival of ours, perhaps?"

It had occurred to me, yes. But I was too ready to spill Hektor's blood, and it wasn't until my own blood had cooled that I started to think. Best not to tell him that, though. I can't have anyone knowing that the dead man was my fiancée's pimp.

"Why did you kill those people, Vladi?" David asks, fixing me with a stare.

The best way to lie is to disguise it amongst truths. I'm less likely to give myself away if most of what I say is factual.

"Because one of them threatened my wife-to-be, Morgana," I say. "You'll meet her tomorrow. She's the daughter of George Bloom. I collected her, then called on Hektor to warn him off. He wouldn't listen, so I took decisive action."

David narrows his eyes. "Your father insists you marry, and you rock up with a bride the same day? Impressive. How did you get her to agree?"

"George owed money to Niko the Flea. I cleared the debt so George would owe me instead, and when that wasn't enough incentive, I told Morgana I'd kill her father if she resisted."

David sips his drink and grins at me. "Diabolical. I like it. You think you can trust her?"

"What can she do?" I shrug. "Her parents' lives are in the balance. I think she'll stay in line."

"Whatever you say." David gets to his feet. "But I'll bet you didn't tell your father about the murder pit stop you made on the way home. Be more careful, Vladi."

I nod. "I'll look into it, *dyadya*, and take responsibility for any consequences."

"You're a good boy, Vladi." David pats my shoulder. "Remember, you have a lot to prove. Don't let pussy cloud your judgment, or your enemies will think you're whipped and not up to the job. Nothing makes you more of a puppet than love."

Papa said as much a thousand times. My grandfather did a number on both of his sons. That doesn't mean he was wrong, though.

Where would we be today if Papa had allowed his heart to rule him? Impossible to say, but I doubt we'd be as wealthy or powerful as we are.

Love may be sublime, but the cost is great.

"Don't worry," I say. "I have neither the time nor inclination to get to know Morgana. We have nothing in common. She hates me, too, which helps."

We walk into the foyer, and the sight of Lilyana's piano reminds me of things I prefer to forget. Long-buried memories are pricking my consciousness this evening, and if I dwell on them, I'll sink into an apathetic funk instead of attending to my responsibilities.

"I'm going to see your father," David says as we ascend the stairs. "I won't mention this to him. But I hope you have your head on straight, for all our sakes."

"I'm not gonna choose a woman over our empire. My duty will always come first."

David's words echo in my mind as I head for the kitchen.

My uncle is on my side. But he's got some gall to insinuate that killing Hektor was some kind of tantrum.

I fucking hate vice. Papa always encouraged it—it's easy money and doesn't require a lot of manpower to manage, but it's a dirty, cheap business. I don't want unknown junkie pimps throwing their weight around. Is that so unreasonable?

I'm something of a hypocrite, given that my deal with Morgana isn't a million miles removed, but I don't care.

For twenty years, I built our business interests so we could hide our less legitimate dealings, and I was almost a recluse. I didn't have relationships that lasted longer than a couple of dates.

But Papa couldn't resist a final twist of the knife. He loves his bratva just a little more than he hates me. After all my sacrifices, he still wants me bound to a loveless marriage like his own.

Love is fucking pointless. It doesn't last and can turn any powerful man into a broken shell. I've worked too hard to be undermined by a pretty little redhead with a smart mouth and legs for days.

Morgana is beautiful and intriguing, but that's all. I felt some regret that she'll never care for me, but that was an unacceptable lapse that I'm chalking up to ego on my part. I just don't like that she isn't fawning over me.

I smile as I take the cold cuts from the refrigerator.

Enemies with benefits. That's a thing, right?

10

Morgana

"So the super-rich guy you met earlier kidnapped you for his bride and casually murdered Hektor and his boys?" Josie asks. "Do I have that right?"

My cell phone is on loudspeaker mode, and I'm in the walk-in wardrobe, checking out the clothing choices. There's a pair of soft palazzo pants in a cool-looking satin and several cashmere tank tops. I pull the hangers from the rail as I speak.

"I know it sounds crazy," I say, "but I don't think Vlad will let anything happen to us. Hektor is gone."

"There'll be trouble, Morgana. Your man is a big shot, but he isn't the only one."

I peel the dress off my body and dump it on the floor, grateful to be rid of it. The pants feel smooth as I pull them over my legs.

"What can I do about it?" I ask, tugging a tank top over my head and shaking my hair loose. "Vlad doesn't seem worried. I'll talk to him about getting you a proper job, away from all that bullshit."

"I'm surprised at how cool you are about this," Josie says. "For someone who's effectively a captive, you're taking it all in your stride. You like him, don't you?"

"Vlad? No. I hate him. He saw something he wanted and took it. He's no better than Hektor, but I'm stuck with it. Again."

"So be careful. I know you and your needy little heart. Jack damn near killed you, and then years later, you fell for the same act from Hektor. You already learned what hell it is to love a toxic man."

I didn't know Josie back then, but I told her the sordid tale from end to end. I hate it when she reminds me of my mistakes, but she means well.

"Please leave it be," I sniff. "I know I look past the bad stuff when I meet someone. But there's no way I'm gonna fall for Vlad. He's a murderer. A blackmailer. An entitled, possessive asshole who needed to hear 'no' a lot more often when he was a kid."

"Okay, if you say so." Josie can tell we're done with the subject. "So what time tomorrow for this wedding dress shopping extravaganza?"

"I don't know. I'll message you. But promise you'll come. I'm in way over my head."

"Of course I will. Try to relax, and I'll see you in the morning."

Josie hangs up, and I feel suddenly alone.

All I wanted was freedom. To pursue my dreams of becoming a photographer and living my damn life. But every choice I made moved me further from that vision.

Thanks, Fate. I was wrecking my life just fine, but no. You had to come along and help.

I really thought Vlad was a hero. He beat up those muggers, sent them packing, flirted with me, and bought me ice cream. So far, so cute.

How could everything have gone *so* wrong since?

I can't let myself fall again. Although Vlad rescued me from Hektor and gave my father a reprieve, he expects me to pay a steep price. I can stand before a congregation and say meaningless words, but that won't make it real.

I will see this through. The real world is waiting for me.

My stomach is growling. It's weird to call for food like the place is a hotel, so I decide to go foraging. After making a couple of wrong turns, I locate the kitchen and open the door to find Vlad at the counter, spreading something on a slice of bread.

"That's not a burger."

"It's for Lilyana," Vlad says without looking at me. "She has had no supper."

"Isn't this the sort of thing you should delegate to the little people?" I ask, a teasing edge creeping into my voice. He raises his eyes to me.

"My sister needs things done a certain way. It's the housekeeper's day off, and I don't trust anyone else."

Vlad's expression is not inviting, and I stay silent as he redirects his attention to the food. It's fascinating to watch because he's so precise. He spreads mustard and mayonnaise on the bread, carefully smoothing the condiments to the edge before arranging pastrami and slivers of Emmental. He removes the crust and cuts the sandwich in half.

"Come with me." He retrieves a can of Coke from the refrigerator. "I rang out for the burgers. Someone will bring them to us when they arrive. You can say hello to my sister."

∼

We take the elevator to the fifth, and Vlad knocks on a door.

"Lili, it's Vladi," he says, his voice warm. "I have some food for you."

A girl opens the door, smiling at Vlad. She looks roughly the same age as Avel, and her skin is pale, with freckles scattered over her nose. Her enormous eyes are the same gray as Vlad's, and she has the family's high cheekbones. I try not to stare at the silver scar from her temple into her hairline.

Lilyana sees me, and a dark cloud passes over her brow.

"This is Morgana," Vlad says. "She and I will marry in a couple of days."

"Hiya, Lili," I say, waving.

"Hello," Lilyana says guardedly. "You're pretty. Do you like the piano?"

I smile at her. "Very much. I hope to hear you play soon."

"At your wedding if you want." She returns my smile with a shy one of her own.

"That'd be wonderful." I hand her the Coke. "I'm going dress shopping tomorrow. You wanna come along?"

Lilyana glances at her brother. He's staring at me, his brows lowered, and she seizes her chance.

"Yes, please." She takes the plate from Vlad's hand. "Thank you for the sandwich, Vladi. May I go shopping with Morgana?"

"If you wish," he says. "Are you alright? Do you need anything else?"

"No, I'm fine. I'll eat and then go to bed. G'night."

She mirrors my coy wave as she closes the door.

11

Morgana

Vlad and I sit on our bedroom balcony, eating burgers and drinking La Croix.

I still think he's an asshole, but I'm dying of curiosity. He's such a contradiction. Which of his faces is the real one?

"I didn't expect to see that side of you," I say. "You're so gentle with Lilyana. Why?"

Vlad leans back against his chair and closes his eyes. "Is this the interview, Morgana? Because I'm not in the mood to spill my life story."

I glare at him. "How am I supposed to play along with this stupid situation you've put me in if you won't tell me anything about yourself?"

Vlad tilts his head, considering my point. "Alright, here it is. Lilyana and Avel are twins. My mother was too old to have more children, but my father never let her use birth control. She died from septicemia after they were born."

A touch of strain creeps into his voice. He struggles to talk about these things, despite his efforts to seem blasé.

"When Lili was five, she fell down a flight of stairs and smashed her head to shit. She was in the hospital for weeks." Vlad puts his burger down as though he's lost his appetite. "My father kept saying if she was hurt that bad, she'd be better off dead."

"That's sick. What is his problem?"

"It would be depressing to dig into why my father is like he is. He would have married Lili off, and he never spoke to her again when he realized no one would want her."

I phrase my next question carefully. "So, what's her situation, exactly?"

"She suffered a multi-site traumatic brain injury. As a result, she has a mild learning delay and some sensory issues. She's shy and self-conscious, and that makes her isolated." He sweeps his hair off his forehead. "Her piano playing went from tinkering to virtuoso within two years. She was playing Bach from memory before she was six."

I smile. "She seems sweet."

"I adore her."

Vlad's eyes are closed, and he looks peaceful for the first time since I met him.

Who the hell *is* he? This kidnapping, murderous criminal who speaks tenderly about his vulnerable little sister and makes her sandwiches just so?

"Anyway," he says, "my father considers Lili to be some kind of shameful secret and rarely even speaks her name. But you invited her shopping with you, just like that. Why?"

"She's struggling to navigate a brutal world," I say. "I understand how she feels. And because I'm *kind* to people, Vladi. It's this new thing the kids are doing now."

"Well, I don't know about that, but I appreciate it," Vlad says. "Her face lit up when you asked."

"No problem. I could use a cellmate. Lili and I can be prisoners together."

"Lili is *not* a prisoner," Vlad snaps. "I look after her. No one understands her like I do, and I'll die before I see the bratva life eat her alive."

"But you'll play the game when you want something for yourself? You want the money and the bratva and will do whatever it takes to get them, but you don't care what you do to *me*. The ends justify the means, right?"

Vlad gets to his feet, shoving his unfinished food into the takeout bag. "Think what you want, *lisichka*. It makes no difference to the situation."

"Wait a minute," I say, scurrying after him into the bedroom. "We have stuff to work out. Where am I gonna sleep?"

"With me."

I stop dead. "We discussed this, Vlad."

He closes the space between us so we're almost nose to nose. I refuse to back away from him, and he bristles at my defiance, snatching my wrist and pinning it to my side.

"Do it, I dare you," I sneer. "It wouldn't be the first time I've been hit. Cover me with bruises just a few days before our wedding. How will that look to your father's buddies, huh?"

Fuck knows where I'm getting the gall to sass him, but I've had enough. Yesterday another rich, entitled man wanted things I didn't wanna give, but this feels different.

"Morgana, you're gonna be my wife. We have to live it, so you'd better get used to having me close."

He's not causing me pain, but his grip is firm. He yanks me closer, and as I bump into his chest, he wraps his arm around my waist, leaning to speak in my ear.

"I'm not letting our first kiss be at the altar. Come on. Show me your best acting, and I'll sleep on the couch tonight."

One swipe of my nails would blind him, but what would be the point?

I watched him make Lili's sandwich with the meticulous approach of a surgeon, and I never thought he was capable of the warmth that came through when he spoke of her. Something in my perception of him has shifted.

It's not a seismic shift by any means. But reality is crumbling away, and hope unfurls like a fragile shoot in the space it leaves behind.

Can something good come of this? Is Vlad truly a monster, or will I marry a man of flesh and blood?

Let's find out.

"If you wanna kiss me, do it," I say.

Without missing a beat, Vlad lowers his lips to mine. His mouth is warm, his tongue teasing my lower lip. His scent is intoxicating, and despite everything, I melt into his arms, sliding my fingers through his hair. He pulls me tight against his body and kisses me deeper, releasing my wrist to slide his hand to the back of my neck. His fingertips massage the nape, and I let out an involuntary moan.

A voice inside screams at me.

Don't, Morgana. He's just a sexy, toxic, controlling bastard. Don't let him get to you. Break it off!

I pull away with a gasp.

Vlad grins. "If you kiss me like that on our wedding day, you're gonna give me a problem that is frowned upon in church."

I feel his erection against me, and I'm appalled to feel my pussy throb in response.

Jesus Christ. I really have a type, don't I?

"You said to give you my best acting," I say, pushing his hands off me. "Either you're easily impressed, or I've missed my calling."

Vlad's expression is hard to read. "A promise is a promise, Morgana. I'll get a shower and make myself comfortable in the lounge. I have somewhere to be tomorrow morning, so I booked the bridal appointment for ten a.m. Sasha will drop you off at the boutique. I'll meet you there and take you for lunch."

Moments ago, I was ready to fight him with claws and teeth for insisting on sharing a bed with me. Now I desperately want him to stay with me. Or on me. In me. Whatever.

"Okay," I manage. "Good night."

After Vlad leaves, I realize I have nothing to wear to bed. No big deal, I guess.

Oh, wait. Shit.

I left my phone in the dressing room.

12

Vlad

I turn on the shower and strip. The ensuite fills with steam, the tension loosening as the warmth eases the ache in my muscles.

I wanted to toy with Morgana because she was pissing me off with her questions, but now I feel like a fool. Something unexpected passed between us, and it can't be undone. As much as I need her to play her role, I don't want her to capitulate entirely. I respect her convictions, and that's an unexpected sensation.

It felt so good to kiss her. Her body was tense in my arms, eyes blazing with anger, yet she gave me her lips. It's so satisfying to *taste* the fight in a woman.

I'm willing to stand beside Morgana at the altar with blood on my hands. Hektor may be dead, but how can I swear to honor and protect my wife if the man who tried to hit her yesterday is still breathing? Vito Serra has zero chance of survival, even if he tells me what I want to know. Once I get what I need, I'll kill him, regardless.

I see a sliver of fabric on the tiled floor. When I stoop to investigate, my breath catches in my throat.

Morgana's panties, if they can be called that. Nothing more than a scrap of peach cotton. I hold them to my nose and inhale deeply.

A fresh, zesty tang. The unique scent of my fiancé's pussy, the pussy I swore never to touch without her consent.

I return to the bathroom and take the panties under the running water. My cock is painfully hard, and I lean against the cool tile, gripping my shaft to relieve the ache.

I never said I wouldn't jerk off to her.

I wrap the panties around my hand, so the part that touched Morgana is rubbing along my length. A moan escapes me as I work my cock, pumping firmly.

Fuck. I'd love to have her on her knees in front of me right now. Watching her eyes widen as I push my cock right to the back of her—

My shaft thickens in my hand, and my knees threaten to buckle as I come. I bow my head, panting as I recover.

The thought of her pushed me over the edge and into bliss. That never happened before, not so quickly.

I thought I was in control, but I'm not sure anymore.

I rinse off and scrub shampoo through my hair, trying to wash my doubt away. Morgana is stunning, and her attitude toward me is refreshingly shitty, but that's no big deal. I like her. So what?

It's fine. She's not getting to me.

~

Morgana

I know I could follow Vlad, but I don't think I should after what just happened between us. Can I trust myself not to jump his bones?

A distant sound of running water. I'm too late. He's in the shower.

I can sleep in these clothes, but there's no way I can relax without my phone beside me, and I left it on top of the vanity unit in the dressing room.

I peer around the door, relieved to see that he is indeed in the ensuite. Steam billows out from a gap in the sliding panel.

Ignore him. Get your phone.

As I reach the vanity, I hear his voice.

"Morgana."

Fuck!

I wheel around and freeze, but Vlad is still in the shower. How did he see me? He couldn't possibly have heard me over the pounding of the water.

Ruined Beauty

His palm appears on the steamed-up glass, water running over it. Behind it, his naked body is a blur. I see a motion I recognize and nearly fall to my knees.

Vlad is saying my name while he—

I clap my hand over my mouth as though I might breathe loudly enough to give myself away. I'm mesmerized, but I force myself to back away toward the door.

If he opens that panel and sees me standing here, anything could happen. He could kill me. Or, more likely, he could fuck me ragged.

I feel a pull deep in my core, and I'm forced to acknowledge the gravity of my predicament.

A murderer is forcing me to marry him. I'm losing my freedom, my agency, everything. But I'm powerfully attracted to the man, and he wants me too.

Most people get turned on by people they *like*, but not me. I hate Vlad's life, everything he stands for, what he's doing to me. Men like him brought my father low and ruined our lives. But pretending to be crazy about Vlad might come all too easily.

A deep, primal moan comes from within the ensuite.

He's coming. While thinking about me.

Look away. Walk away. Run away. Don't just stand here!

Vlad shuts off the shower, breaking the spell. I turn and run back to the bedroom.

∼

I lie in bed and stare at the ceiling. My body is burning up, but I'm not sick. Or maybe I am.

This sexy-as-all-fuck Russian mob boss wants me. *Me*, Morgana Bloom. Could Vladi, of all people, be the first man I ever attracted who has a scrap of decency?

I'd probably find better relationship prospects on Death Row. But my body didn't get that memo, and there isn't a snowball in hell's chance of falling asleep unless I deal with the insistent pulse in my pussy. I glance at the door to check it's definitely closed.

When I slip my hand beneath my waistband, I find my panties drenched. My clit stands proud, desperate for attention, and I move the little hood, shuddering as pleasure warms my abdomen.

Vladimir Kislev. My captor and, soon, my husband. A man who swore not to touch me unless I asked. What would he have done if I'd stepped into that water beside him?

I close my eyes and imagine it.

Vlad doesn't speak. He knows there's nothing to say. His cock is enormous and angry-looking, thick in his hand. He lets go of it to weave his fingers through my hair, pushing me to my knees.

The water rains down, and he hunches slightly to protect me from it. His purple tip is level with my lips, and I open my mouth. He growls and moves his hips, sliding his warm length to the back of my tongue.

I tighten my throat, trying to feel him there, and my pussy clutches in response. My clit throbs under my fingers.

Vlad digs his fingertips into my scalp, holding my head in place to fuck my mouth. He smashes into the back of my throat, and I gag. As he pulls free of me, a thick strand of saliva links him to my lips, and he gathers it in his palm. His hand invades my mouth, thrusting his fingers as deep as possible, shoving my head onto them. I choke and cough. He laughs as he withdraws, rubbing his spit-covered hand over my face.

I don't know where this rough scenario came from. I never had a man treat me that way, not even Jack—he liked to beat me but rejected me sexually. It was about control.

No. Don't think of Jack now. Stay with Vlad.

He yanks me to my feet and slides his hands under my ass, picking me up easily. My back thumps into the chill of the tile wall, and he presses my knees to my chest, exposing my hot pussy. One firm thrust is all it takes, and he buries himself to the hilt.

I can almost feel him inside me, and tension gathers in my core. My pussy spasms as the image throws me into my orgasm, and I grasp around for a pillow, pulling it over my mouth.

I can't remember when I last came so hard. I roll onto my stomach, the mattress cool under my hot skin, and I'm asleep in seconds.

13

Vlad

The couch is comfortable enough. The drapes are open an inch, and the moonlight cuts the darkness like a clean blade.

I usually sleep in boxer shorts, and tonight is no exception. Morgana has her privacy. I'm not making any more concessions.

I've never known real peace at night. If I felt inclined to self-analyze, I'd say it's because I never feel safe, and part of me still thinks nighttime is when the monsters come out.

My father used to laugh at me when I was afraid as a kid. He told me to *be* the monster. Bring the fear, not sit around waiting for it to find me. But when I slept, I saw his face.

Papa would go out until late and raise all kinds of hell. I remember his men bringing him home, bleeding and raging after getting in someone's face. Things are more stable now.

No one has brought a fight to the family in years. But David was right. I may have poked a bear in my haste to ensure Morgana was safe. That's the last thing we need as I take my rightful place as our leader.

My father beat me black and blue in the name of discipline, and I learned the lesson well. If I turn out to be a strong pakhan, all that suffering won't have been in vain. Maybe Papa will still be proud of me yet.

Everything I want is within reach. I *cannot* let a woman distract me.

A noise from the bedroom breaks my train of thought. A muffled cry, quiet at first, then louder. I open the bedroom door.

Morgana is asleep, wearing the same clothes as earlier. I never gave her a chance to get something to wear to bed.

Suddenly, she raises her arm and swats at the air, rolling onto her back. She throws her body so forcefully that she almost falls off the bed.

"No, don't!" she cries. "Stop it!"

Who is she dreaming about? I'm already thinking of all the ways I'll make them suffer, whoever they are. What the *fuck* did they do to her?

"Morgana," I say, sitting on the bed beside her. "Wake up, *lisichka*. You're safe. It's just a nightmare."

Morgana's mouth is open, her face frozen in fear. I grab both shoulders and lean over her, jostling her harder.

"Morgana!" I pull her upright. "Wake up!"

Her eyes fly open, but she's not looking at me. She scans around, searching for unseen demons. I let go of her and click my fingers in her eye line.

"Here. Focus."

Her eyes meet mine, and she slaps me with such force that I almost fall off the bed.

"Jesus fucking *Christ*!" I catch her wrist as she pulls back to hit me again. "Enough, dammit!"

My ear is ringing. Morgana whispers some jumbled words, but I can't hear her properly. She's shaking, her skin coated in a sheen of perspiration, and she collapses onto my chest.

I wrap my arms around her and pull her onto my lap. She rests her cheek on my heart and locks her feet at the small of my back, whimpering quietly. I drag the duvet over and wrap it around her, trying to warm her up.

Incredibly, she's still asleep, but she's clinging to me like a baby monkey, and I feel like I've seriously overstepped.

For all I know, it's *me* who haunts her nightmares tonight.

I reach for her hands and try to pull them away from my neck, but she tightens her grip. God knows why I can't bring myself to shove her off me, but I can't sit cross-legged all night, either. I'm forty-five. I'll be crippled by morning.

I maneuver until I can lower us both onto our sides. She relaxes a little as her body sinks into the mattress, and I pull the duvet under her chin.

What am I doing? The sooner I can sneak away, the better.

I fumble at my watch, trying to shut off the alarm. Light is streaming in from the lounge.

Wait a minute. Did I *sleep*?

I rub my eyes and recheck the time. *Yep*. It's six-thirty a.m. I lay beside Morgana, closed my eyes, and got seven-and-a-half hours of rest. The last time I slept that long was after Lilyana's accident when I went through my Valium phase.

Morgana is still out for the count. I watch her body move with each breath.

Get out of here.

I slide out of bed and make for the door.

"You asshole." Morgana rolls over and opens her eyes. "How *dare* you sneak into bed beside me while I was asleep? We made a deal. Why should I trust you to keep your word about *anything*?"

For once, her anger at me isn't justified. I could tell her she was in distress, how she wrapped herself around me and wouldn't let go. But I say nothing.

She never meant to show her vulnerability to me, and she's in a powerless position already. Better to let her be mad. It's not like it changes anything.

"Sorry, *lisichka*." I smile and shrug. "But we'll be married in a couple of days. I can't have you getting used to your space."

Morgana clears her throat. "It doesn't matter how close you get," she says, tapping her temple with her fingertip. "You can never get in here. Or," she places her palm over her heart, "*here*. I've had experience with men like you, and I know what you are. Spoil me, humor me. I don't care. You don't own me."

My indulgence of her will be my undoing. I know it. Just seeing her eyes flash with defiance makes me want to wreck her. If I fucked her sassy mouth hard enough, she'd think twice about giving me all this static.

"Yes, I do," I say. "My parents taught me to put my name on my possessions, and by marrying you, that's exactly what I'll be doing. Enjoy dress shopping, and I'll see you for lunch."

14

Morgana

Something is happening here.

Does Vlad know what I did last night? He was unfazed by breaking his promise to me. And he manipulated me into kissing him.

Even if that's true, I wanted it. And seeing Vlad leaning against the doorframe in nothing but his jockeys, smirking at my anger, was... *something*. I didn't know where to look.

He's toying with me, knowing he has all the power. Or does he? He moaned my name as he jerked himself off. Maybe I have a more substantial effect on him than I thought. He sure as hell wanted to show me that chiseled body.

I close my eyes, trying to block out the memory of his powerful chest, tapering to his lean waist and the narrow strip of hair drawing my eye toward his—

Enough. Even if Vlad is not a man to keep his promises, I'm in no position to act out. I have places to be.

I throw on jeans and a slightly too-small crop top. A devilish thought occurs, and I check the wardrobe. Sure enough, Vlad's shirts are hanging there, crisp and white. I put one on, and it swamps me, but it looks cute when I tie it at the waist. There are several boxes of tennis shoes in different sizes, and I quickly find the ones that will fit. I have little makeup except what's in my purse, but a quick swipe of peachy lip balm makes me look reasonably put-together.

Vlad's aftershave is beside the basin. I spritz it into the air, walking through the scented cloud, the familiar fragrance of my husband-to-be settling on my skin.

I'm still afraid, but it's not the only emotion jostling for space in my mind. A lascivious spike of curiosity has skewered my imagination, and despite my ridiculous predicament, I can't deny my desire for him.

Honestly, Morgana. You should be able to learn from negative conditioning. You're one down to a lab rat.

I used to have a life. I went to parties, all that stuff. I met Jack at a bar, and we hit it off immediately—he was so confident and funny. Before we'd been together a month, he talked about marriage, kids, and a house. I thought I was lucky to meet a man ready for commitment, so I moved into his apartment, and all was well. Then it wasn't.

Jack began to criticize me. It started with small things, like questioning my choice to wear a pretty dress when I was only meeting friends. That kind of thing. Then he'd give me the silent treatment if I ate anything unhealthy, saying I was 'letting myself go.' He wanted me to dye my hair blonde, but I refused.

The first time he hit me was on my twenty-first birthday. I wanted to go out and have a few drinks, but he didn't. I capitulated, but it wasn't enough for him. After a four-hour argument that left me confused and exhausted, I tried to go, and he back-handed me with no warning. His signet ring cut my brow bone, and I was severely bruised. I stayed home for days after, not wanting anyone to see my injuries.

Vlad has a veneer of respectability, obscene amounts of money, and the power that comes from living a life unrestrained by morals, ethics, or the word of law. But under all that, he's another charming, handsome mess with severe control issues.

And judging by my insistence on fantasizing about him, I have learned *nothing*.

~

I find my way to the kitchen and find Lilyana eating maple bacon pancakes. A woman stands at the skillet, her back to me.

"Good morning, Morgana," Lilyana says. "This is Dulcie, our housekeeper."

Dulcie smiles and wipes her hands on her apron. "Hello. Would you like some pancakes? No one eats them except Lili, but I've made too many as usual."

"Thanks, I'll take a couple."

I join Lili at the table, and Dulcie sits too. She pours my coffee first before fixing a cup for herself.

"I'll eat the last few," she says. "Mr. Kislev doesn't like waste. Sergey, that is. I look forward to my Vladi being the master of the house."

"Is Sergey tough to work for?" I ask, adding sugar to my coffee.

Dulcie frowns. "He's not a pleasant man. And I should know—I've worked for the family for almost fifty years." She sees my expression and laughs. "I know, *bella ragazza*. I am youthful, no?" She tosses her hair like a model, drawing a giggle from Lilyana. "Vladi's mother, Stefania, brought me from Italy as her maid. I was eighteen, and she was a little older. She married Sergey at her father's behest to prevent a war between her family and his."

What a world they live in. Lives hijacked in the name of money and power.

"So you've known Vlad his whole life?"

"Yes." She sighs. "He was his mother's heart. She didn't have love in her marriage, so she poured it into her boy, and his father resented them both for it. They had something he envied and despised, and although Sergey tried, he couldn't ruin it. Not while Stefania was still alive, anyway."

I glance at Lilyana. It must be tough for her to hear about the mother she never knew.

"Anyway," Dulcie says, getting to her feet, "I will tell Sasha you're almost ready to go. An important day for you!"

Her kind face instills me with courage, and I ask a bold question.

"Your mistress was forced to marry into this family, and you know how she suffered. Yet you seem delighted for me. Aren't I in exactly the same boat?"

Dulcie smiles. "You are not, *mia caro*. Things will be different for you."

"Why?"

She puts her hand over mine. "Because no matter how hard he tries, Vladi is not his father. You'll see."

15

Vlad

Serra is at breakfast. The fat bastard isn't intelligent enough to vary his habits, so it took Arman less than ten minutes to find out where he'd be this morning.

I'm wound up, and killing Serra will make me feel better, but I won't accost him in the restaurant. I need privacy.

Morgana has me messed up. I could have silenced her in seconds this morning if I'd told her what happened last night. She was so vulnerable, so different from the spitfire of a girl I'd been tussling with. Humiliating her into compliance would make my life much easier, so why didn't I press my advantage?

The truth pushes to the front of my mind, refusing to be denied.

Because I don't *want* to crush her. I crave the challenge. She doesn't want me, but I'm obsessed with changing her mind.

Serra appears in the restaurant's doorway, wiping egg yolk from his mouth with his sleeve. He crosses the road in front of my parked car and gets into his own, pulling away from the curb. I move into the traffic behind him, a safe four cars back.

I don't know if he would recognize me, but I know him—he's a nasty, petty crook who will shift anything for the right price. A couple of years back, he tried to sell one of our shipments from under us, and Sasha gave him one chance to admit it before kicking the ever-loving shit out of him. I don't know what's happening here, but I need to get to the bottom of it and not sleepwalk into a disaster.

A short drive brings us to a townhouse just off Columbus Avenue. I drive past to allay suspicion, and Serra's car is parked outside when I return. He's at the front door, fumbling for a key.

I lurk, waiting until he gets the door open, then rush him, slamming into his back. He grunts as he hits the floor, and I close the door.

"Vito Serra, good morning. Do you know me?"

Serra rolls over and squints. Recognition flashes in his eyes.

"What the fuck is your problem?"

This man tried to beat Morgana. There's no fucking way he's gonna survive an encounter with me, but I need him to believe otherwise at first.

I grasp his collar and drag him to his feet, dumping him at the bottom of the stairs. "My brother Sasha didn't convince you to stay away? Wait until I tell him. He thought he'd been too soft on you last time. How long did you wear that neck brace?"

"Three months," Serra squawks, trying to stand. "I learned my lesson. I'm not up to anythin'. Just hangin' out with new friends."

"Like Hektor?"

Serra frowns. "Yeah. He's one of yours, right? He was meant to send me a girl yesterday, but he didn't even answer his phone."

The urge to pound his face until it looks like ground beef is hard to resist. Instead, I kick him hard in the ribs, winding him, and he collapses again.

"Hektor was not one of ours."

"Look, I don't know what he's playin' at, but it ain't nothin' to do with me." Serra draws a deep, wheezing breath. "I don't know him personally. I like pretty whores. That's it."

"Do you have a favorite?"

Serra blinks stupidly at me. He leans against the balustrade and regards me warily. "Uh, yeah, I do. Redhead girl."

"I like a redhead. Is she a good fuck?"

"I didn't get to find out," Serra says. He returns my grin, thinking he's on safe ground. "She wouldn't let me fuck her, so I tried to teach her a lesson, but the hotel people stopped me. I shoulda got another go on her, but she never showed." His face suddenly collapses as though he's thought of a possibility. "I don't know where *she* is, either. Like I said, nothin' to do with me."

"Vito, Hektor is dead. I killed him. If you have any sense in your fat head, you'll tell me who he worked for, so I can take it up with his boss."

"I don't know!" Serra whines. "I'd tell you. You know I'm a coward."

This is a fair point. Killing Hektor might be intimidation enough for whoever was holding his leash. But regardless of what Serra knows, he's a loose end.

"Aren't you gonna invite me in, Vito? Let's have some coffee."

Serra scurries ahead of me. "Kitchen's this way. We can talk it over. I could help somehow."

I loosen my tie and pull it over my head.

"Whatever you say."

I grab a fistful of Serra's hair and throw the loop around his neck. My knee comes up between his legs, and he folds to the ground, landing face-down. I sit on him and wedge my heels under his shoulder blades, pulling the loose end of my tie.

The leverage makes throttling him easier. Serra splutters and gasps as the ligature squeezes his windpipe.

"That girl you tried to beat and fuck," I snarl, "is *my* fiancée. You deserve to die a thousand times over for even looking at what's mine, but," I yank hard, and Serra's neck makes a cracking sound, "I have things to do today."

Serra's squirming gives way to a feeble shudder, and a large patch of piss spreads on the floor. I grimace and climb off him, leaving my tie in place around his neck. His eyes are bloodshot and bulging.

So that's that for now. Arman is keeping his ear close to the ground. If I get any more information, I'll act on it.

Now to trickier business. After all, I'm getting married tomorrow, and although I left the boutique owner with explicit instructions, I'm sure Morgana is making trouble by now.

I lock the door and post the keys through the mail slot.

16

Cassius

Whoever cleaned did an excellent job. Bare floorboards, the empty frame of the coffee table where the glass was smashed. The couch is stained and punched with a bullet hole, but that's it.

There's a CCTV camera above the door, but on closer inspection, it's a decoy.

Hektor, Hektor. You cheap bastard. It's no wonder someone sauntered in and murdered him.

I had no particular regard for Hektor. The first time I met him, I thought he was an idiot. The second time, I was fucking sure of it. He reminded me a lot of my father, who beat my mother black and blue to remind her who was boss but never seemed to keep the upper hand. If Hektor had taken a gentler approach, he could have got those whores to love him even as he hurt them.

I don't like women as people. They are not thinkers. I don't even particularly enjoy fucking them, but I do like screwing with their heads. Still, there's nothing like prison to make a man miss pussy.

Ira Trusov is a bratva boss and my employer. I made myself indispensable to him while I was doing time, and the gratitude of a mob boss is a valuable commodity. I took out some of his rivals in the joint, and in return, he funded a crooked appeal.

Now I work for him, and he has given me a specific task—to find out who had the gall to straight-up murder his pet pimp.

Hektor shouldn't have been doing his business around these parts, but that's not the point—someone killed the slimy fuck without opening a dialogue first, and that's just rude.

I sit on the couch, trying to picture the scene.

Our man probably said little. He shot Hektor and whoever else was here but didn't smash the camera. Either he knew it was fake, or he didn't give a shit. Quick, efficient, and cold, just like me. I wonder why he did it. I'll ask before I kill him.

I head outside and walk around, getting a feel for the space. Nothing here except a dented dumpster. There's nothing unusual inside it, just regular street garbage. A patch of concrete stands out on the ground beside it, clean and scrubbed.

The door isn't damaged, suggesting it was open but guarded. Was there an altercation here too?

I scan inside the dumpster again, and this time, I notice a reddish-brown splatter on the inside wall. I brace my arms on the rim and vault inside, cursing as I land in a couple of inches of fetid water. Nothing here but stinking newspapers and rotten food.

I'm about to climb out when I see a small book floating. I grab it and shake the water off.

It's a diary with just a few lines for appointments and essential information. There's a notebook section in the back, and I find names and numbers. I flick back to yesterday's date.

Vito Serra, M, 7 p.m. Drop off and collect.

Perfect. A name is all I need. Whoremongers use the services of more than one girl and more than one pimp. Others in the business will know him.

I take out my cell phone and make a couple of calls. I'll soon find a snitch who'll take a few crisp bills in return for the skinny on Vito Serra.

17

Morgana

"Welcome to Aida's Bridal." The boutique owner waves her arm at the rails. "I have hundreds of dresses here." She looks me over. "You're about a size four? Most samples will fit, but I will adjust your choice for you. I promise it'll be perfect. Oh!" She clicks her fingers. "I almost forgot. Mr. Kislev left you a note about dress styles with the champagne and macarons. If you want anything else, I'm instructed to get it and charge it to him."

"Thanks," I say, trying to hide my irritation. *Style notes? Ha.* We'll see about that.

Josie is fiddling with a bottle. "This is fantastic," she says. "I love champagne, and there's enough to—"

With a pop and a smash, the front of a glass display cabinet falls away. I burst into laughter.

"Charge that to Mr. Kislev, please, Aida."

Aida produces a hand-held vacuum cleaner and sucks up the mess before stalking away, her mouth set in a thin line.

Lili pours a glass and hands it to me. "Thanks for asking me along. I don't get out much. Vladi is so over-protective."

"He loves you, Lili."

Her brow furrows. "I know. But I'm the weak link for him. Everyone knows Vladimir Kislev has a soft spot for his weird little sister, and one of these days, it'll be his undoing. Papa hates me for being useless, but he hates Vladi for loving me even more."

"Surely the Kislev brothers love each other too?"

"They do, but it's different. And they all have their place. Vladi will be in charge soon. Sasha is our muscle and Vladi's right hand, and Avel," she laughs, "well, Avel is learning how to be Bratva rather than just a brat. Even Arman has a job to do. I serve no purpose."

I catch Josie's eye, and she shrugs. What can we say to her? She's a bratva princess, sheltered but deeply vulnerable. Her experiences, like Vlad's, are worlds away from mine.

We look at the dresses, and the subdued atmosphere lifts as we add gown after gown to the 'maybe' rail.

"Wait." Josie wheels around. "Hadn't we better have a look at Daddy Warbucks' instructions?"

I reach for the envelope, but Josie gets there first, grabbing the paper and scanning it quickly. She frowns.

I snatch the letter from her hand.

Morgana,

You will choose a dress with a modest neckline. It will have a full skirt with a train and will not have cutaways or clear panels anywhere except in the back. I do not insist on long sleeves, but a halter neck is unacceptable.

A veil is mandatory, and I will hear no arguments on the matter. Your chosen dress MUST be ivory or champagne, and NOT lace. You will select court shoes to match.

I have no opinion on how you wear your hair, as long as you style it properly. Your jewelry must be silver, pearl, and/or diamond, not oversized or gaudy.

I will pay for anything you want as long as your selections fit my criteria.

I'll call when I'm on my way to meet you, and Sasha will take Josie and Lilyana home.

Yours, Vlad

Fucking asshole. He reminds me of Jack, with his endless opinions on every outfit I wore. I'm pissed that Vlad demanded I 'choose' a wedding dress, only for him to give me a list of requirements that narrows my options to potentially only a handful. At least it'll make it easier to pick.

Lili reads the note over my shoulder. "He likes you more than you think, Morgana."

I turn to look at her. "How can you tell?"

She raises an eyebrow. "If this were just a performance, he wouldn't care what you wore. But he doesn't want you to show your body in a fitted dress. He hates the idea of his father's buddies moving their eyes over what's his."

"That proves nothing. It's just possessiveness. I've seen it before."

Lili shrugs. "Maybe you're right, maybe not. But I *know* him."

Aida returns and helps me into the first dress, a vast poofy monstrosity with a pie-crust collar and long gauze sleeves. I emerge from behind the curtain with a flourish, nearly taking out a standing lamp.

Josie's eyes widen, and she coughs macaron crumbs onto the carpet. "I'm sorry," she splutters, "but you look like you should be haunting an English stately home. Or marrying Dracula."

"I *feel* like I'm marrying Dracula. What about you, Lili? Any thoughts?"

Lili wrinkles her nose. "Should we worry about the designer? Like, who hurt them? Because what is that?"

"Jeez, okay," I laugh. "So it's a no!"

The second dress is even more meringue-like. Aida laces the corset tightly, pressing my boobs against the sweetheart neckline.

Cleavage is as cleavage does. It's gonna happen, no matter what my opinionated fiancé thinks.

A phone is ringing somewhere, and Aida scurries away to answer it. I twirl around in front of my entourage, to hysterical sniggering.

"*That*," Lili trills, "is *far* better. You look like a pirate serving wench. But it'd come in handy if the marquee didn't show." She looks suddenly worried. "How do you pee in a wedding dress, anyway?"

"No more fizz for *you*, young lady. Josie?"

"If I were being diplomatic, I'd say it's interesting."

"And if you were *not* being diplomatic?"

"Then my word of choice would be 'fuckawful.' Look, in all seriousness," Josie swigs her champagne and hiccups, "tell Vlad to go to hell. He's not gonna say anything, not in front of all those people."

She has a point. I may have more power than I think. If Vlad wants to appease his father, he can hardly act like he's anything other than thrilled on the day.

"What if he checks with Aida?" I ask. "He's paying. I can't rely on her to cover for me."

Josie grins. "I have an idea. Let's go back to the rack."

18

Vlad

Aida is hanging a garment bag on a rail.

"Your fiancée chose a dress," Aida says, nodding at the garment bag hanging on a nearby rail. "I made only a few minor adjustments. You'll be able to take it with you when you leave."

I unzip the bag and check it out. To my surprise, Morgana has chosen in line with my requirements. Organza sleeves and an ivory A-line with a flared satin skirt. Pretty and modest.

I hate myself for caring. But I can't bear the thought of other men looking at Morgana with the same wolfish hunger I feel when I'm near her. She's beautiful, and there's no disguising that, but the fewer excuses I have to act out tomorrow, the better.

The girls wheel around simultaneously as I come into the dressing room. They're trying on tiaras, and Lili and Josie wear sage green bridesmaid dresses. Morgana is wearing jeans and, God help me—my shirt.

"This is him?" Josie asks, gawping at me. "Oh, you did *not* lie, Morgana."

About what?

My wife-to-be sidles over to me, and I can tell she made short work of the champagne from her uneven steps. "I chose a dress, Vladi. It's exactly what you wanted. Aren't I a good girl?"

Holy hell. I cannot believe she just threw that out there. If we were alone, I don't know if I could resist fucking her right here.

"Yes, you are," I say, smiling at her. "I looked at the dress before I came in here, and it's perfect. Thank you for doing what I asked and not giving me shit over it."

Something closes down in her face, and I feel a wrench of concern.

It's necessary to marry her. I know what I'm doing is wrong, and I can't take it back now. But I no longer hate the idea. I want her standing there beside me, swearing to be mine. Sure, it's all fake, but damn. It's all I can think about.

Morgana pouts. "You're not supposed to see the dress before the wedding!"

"I won't see it again until you walk down the aisle." I can't help but grin at her outrage. "I didn't get a good look. And besides, it's not as though it's a real wedding, *lisichka*."

"What does," Josie pauses, struggling with the word, "*lisichka* mean?"

"Little fox," Lili says. "Because of Morgana's red hair."

Fuck's sake. I love Lili dearly and can't stay mad at her, but did she have to give that away?

I cough and turn to Josie. "I'm told you need a job?"

Josie nods. "Yes, please. You murdered my employer, and while I'm not complaining, a girl's gotta eat."

"Okay. Bright and early Monday morning at Kislev Enterprises, FiDi. Sasha will set you up."

"Who's Sasha?" Josie asks. "Your P. A.?"

Sasha's head appears around the door. "Fuck, no." He flashes a grin. "Vladi just *thinks* I am."

Josie snatches the tiara off her head as my brother approaches. He has the panty-melting sex appeal that ruins a particular type of girl, and Josie's Betty Page bangs and tongue stud put her firmly in that category. Sasha sees the effect he's having, and I know he's gonna do that thing he does.

"Do you want a ride with me?"

There it is.

Josie's mouth is hanging open, and Morgana nudges her. "In the *car*," she whispers.

"Um, yeah, hi, yeah," Josie stammers. "Let me get changed. These dresses are okay, right, Morgana?"

"Looks more than okay to me," Sasha says. Josie laughs too loudly, and I catch Morgana cringe a little.

"We'll wait outside for you, ladies," I say, spinning Sasha by his shoulder and ushering him out the door.

"That woman is fucking gorgeous," Sasha murmurs. "Bridesmaids are supposed to get laid at weddings, right?"

"Nothing to do with me. Try not to fill the house with her screams on my wedding night. I can do without sibling rivalry in that arena."

"You *wish* you could compete with me." Sasha raises an eyebrow. "I heard screams last night, though."

I'm not about to tell my playboy brother that instead of fucking my fiancée, I was consoling her as she struggled through her night terrors.

Lilyana and Josie appear, carrying their dresses in their own garment bags. Sasha holds the boutique door open.

"I'll take you home first, Lili," he says as he walks behind them. "Josie, you live in Brooklyn, right? I'd have been happy to collect you this morning."

I enter the lounge to find Morgana tidying.

"Leave it," I say. "Aida will clean up after you."

"No one taught you to pick up after yourself?" Morgana shakes her head. "I guess this happens when you're rich enough for your cleaners to have cleaners."

I grab her hand and put the empty champagne glass on the table. "Don't bait me, Morgana. I've got a lot on my mind."

She looks me in the eye, then relents. "So you're in charge. What do you want to do now?"

"You really wanna know?" I pull her closer to me. "Why are you wearing my shirt and," I breathe in deeply, "my aftershave? What are you trying to do?"

"*Trying*?" she says, locking her gaze onto mine. "Or am I succeeding, Vladi? Because I'm annoying, combative, bitchy, ungrateful, and in every way not what a good mob wife should be." She bites her lip. "And you love it. Don't you?"

My arm steals around her waist. "Guess what I did for you this morning."

"What?"

"I killed Vito Serra."

Morgana tries to pull away, but I grip her tightly, pressing my body against hers. She loses her footing slightly, and I catch her ass in my hand.

"You're crazy!" she gasps. "You can't just murder people and then say you did it for *me*. I never asked you to."

"Who is gonna stop me, *lisichka*? We're paid up with the law. Our rivals know to keep out of our business. So if I wanna make some loser scream apologies while I bleed the life out of them, then burn the corpse in front of their loved ones—well, yeah. I can fucking do that."

Morgana's hand is in my hair, the other under my shirt, fondling my hipbone. I wonder if she even knows she's doing it. My cock thickens as I hold her in place.

"You wanna know what I think?" I say, taking her chin in my hand and looking into her eyes.

"What?"

"You want to hate me and everything I am, everything I stand for. But you *don't*. Who else can do what *I* do? I'm a man who will kill for you, and it turns you on."

Morgana closes her eyes, her lips parting. I draw in her breath as I lower my mouth to hers.

Aida opens the door. "Mr. Kislev, I just made up the bill for you. Would you like to—" She stops when she sees us. "I'm sorry. I should have knocked."

Morgana has already retreated. Her cheeks are flushed, but she won't look at me.

I pay the invoice without even looking at the balance due. Any amount is worth it.

19

Morgana

We're alone on a private restaurant rooftop overlooking Central Park South, and Vlad is pouring sparkling water from a carafe.

"Here," he says. "You're tipsy. Get your head on straight."

I'm reeling. Whether it's from the bubbly or his attention is hard to say. Why does all my common sense desert me when he takes control?

"Thanks." I take the drink and sip it.

"You know, you needn't make a fool of yourself," he says. "You wanted me to kiss you. It couldn't have been more obvious. I told you already—I'm more than happy to fuck you if that's what you want. It's unnecessary to make a performance out of trying to get my attention."

The *nerve* of this man.

He murdered five people in twenty-four hours because they were causing me problems. He kissed me last night and left me burning, then jerked off in the shower while moaning my name. Not half an hour ago, he grabbed my ass and pressed his cock against me, leaving my pussy throbbing and soaked. And he has the gall to act like *I'm* the one who's going crazy for *him*?

The intelligent bit of my brain that tries to protect me from my stupidity is AWOL. The rest of me wants to ride Vlad until his eyes roll back in his head. I'm sure I wouldn't be so hot for him if I didn't hate him, but it's how my idiot brain is wired. Wicked men with bad attitudes do it for me every time, but they always hurt me in the end.

I rationalize it by telling myself that if I fall in line with Vlad's plans, he's less likely to hurt anyone I care about. I'll get out of this situation quickly and with minimal collateral damage. It's the best way to ensure my parents' safety.

Yep. That's it. It's about survival. So why can't I resist running my mouth?

"You want me more than you're willing to admit," I say, "so drop the take-it-or-leave-it act. I'm sure you could have all the anonymous sex you desire, as long as you don't actually speak to the woman in question."

"Charming." Vlad drapes his arms over the back of the couch. "For your information, I don't fuck around. I'm a billionaire and the heir to a bratva throne, which makes me a prime target for the classic baby trap. So I don't trust anyone."

I can't help but laugh. "So if someone wants to sleep with you, they must have an ulterior motive?"

He shrugs. "I can't be certain they don't. So I keep my dalliances to a minimum."

"And your shower masturbation to a maximum?"

Shit. That's way too close to the mark.

I fill the silence. "You know, because men do that. Less mess."

Vlad knows I'm thinking about him jacking off, and he grins. "You're right. And I'm nothing if not efficient."

A server appears, brandishing a tray.

"Thanks," Vlad says, shooing him away. He takes the cover off the platter, releasing a spicy aroma. "Jambalaya with king prawns," he says. "Nothing too heavy." He scoops rice into a bowl, and I grab a spoon, grateful for something that might take away the bubbly emptiness in my stomach. We fall silent for a few minutes as we eat.

"You know, when we first met, I thought you were a knight in shining armor."

Vlad snorts. "Seriously. How wrong can you be?"

"I'm wondering about that, but not for the reasons you might think. Lilyana seems to believe there's more to you than this cold, sardonic persona you're playing up. Dulcie said the same."

His shoulders stiffen. "I have obligations to my family, Morgana. That means my heart cannot rule me. I keep my emotions under tight control."

"If you say so. But this so-called pretend marriage is getting to you, isn't it? You like me, and you think that might make you seem weak. Am I right?"

Vlad sighs. "Yes. But it's superficial, Morgana. You look good, you feel good. I like the fire in your belly. I'll be proud to have you at my side, and marrying you is no hardship, but don't dig any deeper. You won't find anything good. Lock away your heart as I have, and we will both get through this unscathed." He leans against the couch and tips his head back, closing his eyes. "Who knows?" he adds, his tone unconvincing. "Maybe it'll be fun."

My head is spinning. The fizz is hitting hard now I'm out in the fresh air.

Vlad had his mother's adoration but at a high cost. Now she's gone, he only has his father's warped interpretation of love. He's forgotten how beautiful it can be, and I'm sad for him.

Shouldn't do this. *Fuck it.*

I shuffle close and tuck myself under Vlad's arm. His eyes fly open, and he looks down at me.

"Damn, you're beautiful," he says. "Tell me you hate me. I need to hear it."

"I hate you, Vladi." I slip my fingertips between his shirt buttons and touch his chest. "I really fucking hate you."

Vlad's hand darts in front of me and cradles my throat. He pushes me onto my back, and he's on top of me, his lips crushing mine. I gasp as his tongue delves into my mouth, his hand sliding under the hem of my shirt.

"Tell me not to fuck you." He pins me with his weight, his lips close to my ear. "Tell me not to, and I won't."

My clit presses against the seam of my jeans, and I feel his hardness as he moves his hips. I should say something, but I can't. My panties are so wet, and all I want is for Vlad to pull down my jeans and fill my pussy with his cock.

"Come on, *lisichka*," he murmurs against my shoulder. "You don't want me? Then stop me."

This isn't right. I'm supposed to hate him.

I break our kiss and push at Vlad's chest. "No, I don't want you. Please stop."

Vlad sits back on his heels. "I don't believe you," he says, "but a promise is a promise."

How did he make me forget myself like that? I could blame the alcohol and say he took advantage of me, but it'd be a lie. I wanted to get close to him—it was my stupid fault. Honestly, I thought he would push it, and I could pretend to myself that I never had a choice.

I sit up, smoothing my hair. "Let's get out of here," I say. "I don't want to play these games with you."

Vlad points at the tent in his pants. "Okay. But you'll have to give me a minute."

20

Cassius

Serra's car is outside his house, but he doesn't answer the doorbell. Time to hang back. A talk with Trusov is overdue—he's called me four times already.

Until recently, Trusov kept his dealings concentrated around Chicago. Hektor went to NYC as our emissary to do favors and make friends. Learn who the important people are. But someone murdered him before he'd gotten anywhere. Luckily, I have a few acquaintances in the city.

Niko the Flea was a no-mark when I saw him last, but now he manages loans and collections for various mob clients. He was happy to direct me to Serra and give me some helpful information about the more prominent players.

I find a coffee place and order an espresso. It's late for coffee, but I have a job to do, and I don't intend to rest until I get a handle on it.

Trusov answers after two rings. "You'd better have some good news for me," he says, sounding irritable.

"I'm gonna talk to this guy Serra when he gets home. He has some modest connections, but he's nobody. If he killed Hektor, he's got some gall. What do you want me to do?"

Trusov chuckles. "There's a reason I got you out of prison and installed you in my bratva. You made my life a ton easier. So go do what you do best, my boy."

My father always said I'd amount to fuck all. He used to call me a little bitch, a weakling. One who would always follow and never lead. What did he know? I have what I always wanted—a prominent role in a crime syndicate. The money is useful, but it's not why I'm here. I want to be *feared*. *Respected*.

Did I do some horrible shit to get this far? *Sure.* That's why I'm a good fit in the culture.

"I put the word out amongst the scumbags I ran with in the old days," I say, sipping my coffee. "They'll let me know if anyone mentions Hektor. When I've finished with Serra, we'll better understand the state of play."

"I want this dealt with quickly." Trusov's tone is sharp. "Swift, severe, and without mercy. Is that clear?"

"I understand, Boss."

∼

Serra's doorbell echoes inside, but I hear no footsteps.

I peer through the window. A hand is on the floor in my eye line.

I make my move. One firm kick is enough, and the flimsy door splinters around the lock. You'd think Serra would be more security conscious.

Serra's body is waxy-looking. Purplish patches have formed where his limbs touch the ground, a necktie is pulled under his chin, and the capillaries in his eyes have burst. I squat and prod the man's flabby neck, watching the color recede under pressure. He hasn't been dead long.

This is inconvenient.

Some fucker got here first. What should have been a fact-finding exercise is becoming a pain in the ass.

What do I actually *know*? Who might have had an issue with Hektor that warranted killing him?

I sit back on my heels and think. Whoever killed Hektor and his goons disposed of them quickly, so if the same person is responsible for Serra's death, I should wait and see who comes by.

It doesn't take long to clean the few surfaces I've touched; I don't expect the cops to take an interest, but I'd prefer not to tangle with them.

My car is comfortable enough, and I lie back and wait. After an hour, a van pulls up, waking me from a light sleep. I stay low so I can watch without being seen.

Six men get out and unload cleaning supplies. They are inside the house for twenty minutes, and two men carry a body bag when they emerge. They fling it into the van's rear, loading their gear and snapping off their latex gloves before driving away. Whoever they were, they were clearly under orders.

I thought I would find Hektor's killer and make an example of him. I can do without Trusov deciding I'm not up to the job.

Back to the drawing board.

21

Vlad

I'm barely through the door before Arman appears from the downstairs lounge, beckoning me.

"A minute, Vladi."

Morgana is already halfway up the stairs, desperate to escape me. She and I tried to continue the day, but it was awkward. The conversation was stilted, and in the end, I just stayed in my car while she placed orders in different stores. Her shopping will be delivered later, so at least she has everything she needs, but damn. I wanted to enjoy spoiling her, but it's all becoming too real, and it's getting to her.

"Morgana. Where are you—"

"Go deal with business, Vlad," she says without turning around. "I don't feel well. Too much champagne."

Yeah, right.

I shouldn't have done what I did at the restaurant. We're getting married tomorrow, and Morgana looks like she'd be happier walking to the gallows than down the aisle.

I join Arman in the lounge. I don't have the right to be mad at him for doing the job I asked him to do, but his timing is fucking atrocious.

"You're not the only one asking about this Hektor guy," Arman says as he sits. "The bar owner had a visit from a man he'd never seen before, asking who might want Hektor dead. He didn't know shit, but it didn't stop the stranger from breaking three of his ribs."

"Oh, fucking great," a voice says. David is standing in the doorway, glaring at us. "We have a big problem here, don't we?"

Arman nods. "We don't know who you pissed off, Vladi. They haven't established who killed Hektor, but my inquiries will *lead* them to you. It only takes one scumbag to mention I've been asking, and he'll put two and two together."

I raise an eyebrow. "We're the most powerful bratva in this city, Arman. Once this asshole realizes his mistake, he'll return to his boss with his tail between his legs."

"You'd better hope you're right," David says.

I ignore him and address Arman. "I don't care if this guy *does* come to me. Saves me doing all the running around. We'll pay him off, pay off his boss, whatever." I fix my gaze on David. "Hektor was just a pimp. He wasn't valuable enough to fight over. I'm sure of that."

David and Arman leave without another word.

∾

I stare out the window, watching the dusk drawing in.

I'm glad I kept to myself about Serra. I can do without *dyadya* David telling tales to Papa, and Sasha isn't the only one who can call in a cleaning crew. The less my siblings know, the better.

I will *never* apologize for killing Hektor, Serra, or anyone who offends my wife. The circumstances are irrelevant—hurt her, and it's over. I don't know what made her cling to me in the night, but if fear has a face, I will rip it from his skull.

The room grows dark. Here is peace, if only for now. Meanwhile, my father keeps breathing only out of spite, and tomorrow I will marry a woman who hates me just to appease him. I stare at his velvet portrait, the hated eyes staring straight back.

I will be pakhan. I'll have the control and power I earned through suffering. And I will be like my Papa.

I allow myself a bittersweet smirk. *What an achievement.*

A melodic tinkling cuts through my thoughts. Lilyana is at the piano.

I lean against the doorframe so I can see her better. She's lost in the music, her fingers floating over the keys. She's at her most tranquil when she plays, her anxiety quelled by the security of the instrument she knows so well.

A creak on the stairs, and through the gaps in the balustrade, I see Morgana. She hasn't noticed me, and as I watch, she drifts into the foyer, sitting near the piano. She leans against the back of the chair and closes her eyes.

I don't know why, but my heart aches like never before.

Why must beauty always be ruined?

My mother is dead and gone, and she took her love with her—the love that stopped me from suffocating. After that, the world felt so cold. I don't do enough to keep Mama's memory alive because it hurts me too much to think of her, but pushing her away made space for my father's bullshit to consume me.

She would want me to take care of the family. I can't fail her. Lili almost died because I shirked my responsibilities.

I have no choice. But I *can* choose to be a good husband. I may not be able to love Morgana the way she deserves, but I don't have to hurt her, either.

"Oh, hey, Vladi!"

Lilyana has seen me, and she stops playing and waves at me. Morgana's expression is cool, her eyes refusing to be caught.

"Hey, Lili. Sorry. I didn't want to disturb you."

"I was about to practice your wedding song," Lili flexes her fingers. "You said I could play anything I wanted, right?"

"Right."

Morgana is on her feet. "I'm gonna go to bed," she says, avoiding looking at me.

"No, stay. You and Vladi have to dance tomorrow—Sasha told me Papa expects it. I'll play, and you practice dancing."

"Okay," Morgana says. "One dance."

I join her in the open space before the piano, and Lili flicks on a standing lamp. Morgana's hands shake as she rests them on my shoulders, and I take hold of her waist, pulling her closer.

Lilyana plays the song I love most in the world. The one I hoped she wouldn't choose.

A hollow feeling fills my chest.

It's only a song. Only a dance. Only a marriage.

It means nothing.

22

Morgana

'*Can't Help Falling In Love.*'

My father used to play the Elvis version when I was a kid, and he made me laugh with his hokey dance moves.

We were so carefree back then. Does Vlad have similar memories to hold on to, or has his mind been consumed with the brutality of his world?

Vlad hesitates, then moves, leading me through slow, swaying steps. He looks lost, somehow, as though he isn't really there behind his eyes.

"Vladi. Are you alright?"

"Yes, *lisichka*. I'm fine."

I glance at Lilyana, but she's miles away, her eyes closed. I lower my voice, leaning close to whisper in Vlad's ear.

"I only agreed to dance because I didn't want to disappoint Lili. She seems determined to believe that you and I could have something real."

"She's a romantic," he says. "She doesn't think she'll ever have a love of her own, but she wants me to be happy so badly. It's her nature to find the beauty in things. My mother was the same." He pauses as though unsure whether to finish the thought. "Maybe Lili sees something we don't."

Vlad and I have known each other only briefly, but beneath the superficial attraction, I'm starting to understand him.

His world is cold, unemotional, and aggressive, and he thinks he must be the same. But he's not *just* his father's son. He's his own man, an individual. It may terrify him, but there's no getting away from it—Vlad *feels*. He feels deeply, and no amount of abuse from Sergey could change that.

"Why do you want to be pakhan?"

Vlad frowns. "This may be hard for you to understand, but my father subjected me to a ton of pain to harden me to the realities of leading a bratva family. By the time I was too big to be beaten, I'd taken his teaching to heart. Under his leadership, my family prospered, and he didn't love *anyone*. He did terrible things but he put the family first."

"You care about the bratva, Vlad." I squeeze his shoulder. "I see that. But you don't have to be your father; you might tear yourself apart trying."

"I don't know how else to be. It's the way of things—those who care always lose. My Mama adored her children, but she paid for it. My father saw to that. She died fearing for her newborns, so I did my duty and looked after all my siblings, especially the twins."

"That's *not* duty," I say. "It's love. And you're too protective of Lili. If you gave her some freedom, I'm sure she'd come into herself and be happier."

Vlad is watching Lili as she plays, his expression serene. She finishes the piece, and as the last note fades, he lets go of me.

I've said too much.

Liliyana stands and yawns. "I'm going to go to bed," she says. "I wanna be fresh for tomorrow. The boys will be drunk, so I'm staying out of it."

Vlad groans. "Ah, yeah. I forgot about that." He turns to me and smiles apologetically. "Sasha refuses to take no for an answer, so we're going out on the town. We'll be out early tomorrow, and the wedding car will collect you ladies at noon."

I can imagine what a bratva bachelor party looks like. Vlad is the incoming pakhan of the city's most prominent Russian mob family. He will probably fuck his way through every expensive hooker between here and Huntington.

"Fine. Well, you enjoy that," I say. My voice is more brusque than intended, and I realize I haven't asked an important question. "Where are we getting married, anyway?"

"Saint Nicholas Russian Orthodox Cathedral, same as my parents," Vlad replies. "The heavy religious atmosphere isn't my bag, but it's tradition.

Great. I turn away, hoping Vlad didn't see my expression. "I'll get out of your way. Have a fun evening."

∾

The garment bag containing the ugly wedding dress is hanging in the bedroom. I undo the zipper and look it over, hating it all over again. Maybe I should get drunk, too, blot everything out. It wouldn't take much—I've barely sobered up from earlier.

No. A hangover would put the cherry on an already shitty cake.

I'm removing my shoes when I hear a door opening. Vlad is in the walk-in wardrobe, preparing for a night of drinking and whoring.

The thought makes me wanna puke. He's done nothing but mess with my head since he carried me kicking and screaming into his world.

A petty rage burns inside me, and I fling open the door.

"Vlad! Don't think you can sneak into bed with me again tonight!"

Across the lounge, Vlad appears, framed in the dressing-room doorway. He's stark naked.

I squeal and cover my eyes. "What are you doing?"

"I live here, and I'm getting dressed. It's courteous to respond when a lady speaks, right?"

"Yes. But I'm happy to wait a moment while you put your cock away!"

"Why?"

This is ridiculous. I take my hands away from my face and place them on my hips.

"You're being pretty childish now, Vlad."

He leans against the door jamb and raises an eyebrow at me. "Is *that* childish?" he asks, pointing at his junk. "It has some heft, *lisichka*. I'm exhausted from carrying it around all day."

I burst into giggles. I can't help it. He dresses, leaving his shirt unbuttoned just enough to show the edge of his chest plate tattoo, and my mouth goes dry. He's so fucking *beautiful*. It should be illegal. How can he be even sexier with his clothes *on*?

"Morgana, listen," Vlad takes my hand. "We're laughing now, and I'm glad, but I know you're pissed about tonight."

I want to deny it, but what's the point? When we danced, all the surrounding bullshit faded away. He felt it, just as I did.

"I'm gonna go out and drink. I'll cringe through a lap dance or two and watch my idiot brothers dancing like morons, but I promise you this." He kisses the back of my hand. "I won't fuck anyone. A man who cheats is no man at all."

"Even in a sham marriage?"

"Yes." He tucks my hair behind my ear. "You might always hate me. Who knows? Perhaps I'll never be able to change that. And I don't know how to do the love thing. But if you want my touch, my body, you only need to ask. I want you more than you can possibly know."

I'm astonished. I never thought he'd keep himself only for me. He could have anyone. Supermodels, actresses. Women who want to be a part of his world.

"Why *me*, Vladi?"

He touches my cheek, his thumb grazing my lip. "You hit me like a train, Morgana. By the time you ruined my suit with ice cream, I was already half-gone. If it weren't for these bullshit circumstances, I'd try to be the man you deserve instead of the messed-up, brutish prick you're stuck with."

"I never fell for a sweet man," I say, wrapping my arms around his neck.

He smiles. "I don't think you realize what my desire really is, *lisichka*. I don't do the lovey-dovey stuff—it's too easy. Other men may have brought you flowers and asked to hold your hand, but once you're mine, I'll kill anyone who looks at you and then fuck you through the damn wall."

That sounds insane, but he doesn't care because he means it. Why is that so *hot*?

"Will you do something for me before you leave?"

"Anything." His lips are on my neck. "Name it."

"Kiss me. And not like the man I deserve. Kiss me like the man you are. Make me understand what I'm getting myself into."

He pulls away and stares at me, searching my face. "You sure? This is your chance to tell me you're joking."

I nod.

Vlad's hand flies to my throat, warm and tight, and he grips it firmly enough to draw a shocked squeak from me. His other hand is under my ass, effortlessly scooping me off my feet. He moves quickly, dumping me on the vanity as he pushes himself between my thighs, and I lose my balance, catching myself on my hands. His lips are hot, his tongue delving into my mouth as he holds my neck like a vise. His other hand massages my hip, slipping beneath my shirt.

I'm shocked at how strongly my body reacts to him. My nipples pebble against his chest, and his hand finds one of the stiff little peaks. He rolls it between his fingers as he moves against me, the friction sends zinging flashes of pleasure through my core.

"I'll keep my promise," Vlad murmurs against my lips, "but I don't have control here, Morgana. No fucking way. You're killing me." He breaks away. "I have to go. The car is waiting. I don't want to finish this only to have to leave you."

"You assume too much. I said a kiss. Nothing else."

"Whatever you say. But will you do something for me?"

I should say no, but fair's fair. "What?"

He grins. "Don't carry on without me. Just hold that thought."

23

Vlad

Sasha, Avel, and I are relaxing for once. It's rare for us to kick back and enjoy each other's company.

This club is not a brothel, but there's very little that money won't buy, especially when we're celebrating. I'm not feeling it tonight, though.

Armen has skipped the festivities. He's prone to paranoia and concerned about the as-yet-undefined threat we may or may not need to deal with. *Dyadya* David is here, but he's killing the vibe.

"Vlad, Vito Serra is dead," David says, slumping beside me. A girl in a tiny leather bikini offers him a shot of vodka, but he swats her away. "Do you know anything about that?"

I take the shot and knock it back. "No," I lie. "And why do you know about it? We don't have any dealings with that asshole anymore."

"Word gets around."

"Who the fuck cares if the fat cunt is dead?" I ask. "Serra was a prick. The only negative consequence I foresee is that the *trattoria* in Little Italy might make less money."

"You know, Vladi," David says, lighting a cigar, "I wonder about you. I'm not sure you have the discipline necessary to be a good pakhan."

Rage grips me. "After everything my father put me through to prepare me for this, you're gonna give me that shit? You have no right, David. You're not my father."

"And *you* are not *him*, either." David raises his eyebrows. "We've been here for two hours, and you haven't touched a single girl."

"Neither has Sasha. I haven't seen Avel in a while, though. Why don't you find him?"

David catches my none-too-subtle hint and takes his leave. Sasha grabs a bottle of Zubrowska and sits beside me, waving at a girl with a platinum-blonde bob and thigh-high boots.

"Calista, get some clean glasses."

"You're about to tell me I shouldn't let David get to me?" I take the bottle from Sasha and unscrew the cap, sniffing.

"He's got too much to say for himself," Sasha says. "But he's an old man. Papa never let David believe he would take control. You know how it is between them—Papa, the favorite son, and David, always trying to prove something. Once Papa is dead, our dear old *dyadya* will calm down. Just put his chair in a sunny spot and make sure Dulcie keeps him in caravan tea, and he'll be fine."

He may be right. David isn't going about it correctly, but he seems highly invested in ensuring I can do the job. It could be less about undermining me than safeguarding the bratva he loves.

"And who knows," Sasha adds, smiling as he takes the glasses from Calista, "perhaps you need him to keep you on track. Look at you now. All these beautiful women want a piece of Vladimir Kislev, billionaire recluse and feared bratva heir, and where are you? Here in body, but in spirit, you're at home with Morgana."

Hearing her name jars me back into the moment. "What?" I ask. "I wasn't listening."

Sasha takes the bottle and pours me a hefty measure. "This is exactly my point, Vladi. What has that girl *done* to you? You've never been bewitched before. I've never even heard you say a woman's name, let alone bring one home."

"You know the deal." I throw back the vodka. It burns momentarily before a smooth, herbal aftertaste warms my palate. "I *have* to get married."

"Yeah, but you chose *her*." Sasha wags a finger at me. "Any mob family would have served their daughter on a platter, but you went for a woman you don't know—and who doesn't know *you*. Why?"

Because she was beautiful and feisty and gave me shit even after I saved her from being attacked? Because her eyes are full of vitality, not dulled from a lifetime of low expectations and endless expensive trinkets? Because she has a brain in her head and fire in her heart?

"I like her, Sasha." I hold out my glass, and he fills it. "Something about her touches me, and it's not just that she's gorgeous, no matter how hard I try to convince myself otherwise." I decide to change the subject. "What's with *you*, anyway? You take girls into the back room two or three at a time. You left your cock at home?"

"Nah." Sasha sounds deflated. "I was ready for a crazy night, but now it seems kinda sordid. Fuck knows where that's coming from."

He's been subdued since he met Josie at the boutique earlier. I suspect he's not so much pining as desperate to screw her, but as she's Morgana's best friend, he's on his best behavior.

David reappears, half-carrying a very drunk Avel. There's a fresh cut on my brother's lip, and he's wearing an idiot grin.

I point at his bleeding mouth. "Who did that?"

Avel slurs as he speaks. "Washn't a big deal. My fault. Liza shaid I couldn't have another girl cuz I'm too trashed. I wuz tryin' to charm her, but I guessh I losht my touch."

Liza's face appears around the door frame. "I'm sorry, Vladi, but that boy doesn't know when to shut up. I slapped him, but my ring caught his lip. Looks worse than it is."

I laugh. Liza is six feet tall with curves for days—a bona fide Amazon. Avel should thank his lucky stars she didn't knock him into next week.

"It's okay," I say, getting to my feet. "Avel can't hold his liquor, but he'll learn. We'll take his stupid ass home where he can't trouble your girls."

"Okay." Liza wags a finger at Avel. "You grow up, Mr. Man. No bratva boy is big enough to show his ass in here. Am I lying, Vladi?"

"No," I say as I wrap Avel's arm over my shoulder. "You hear that, kid? It's way past your bedtime."

"I love you, *brat*," Avel mumbles. "You're such a good brother. Looked after me and Lilyana. Never quit, no matter what Papa..." The words disintegrate into drowsy gibberish.

"We're all done here," I say. "I'm tired. It's gonna be a long day tomorrow, and I'd rather not have my head in my ass."

"Fuck's sake." David catches my eye and grins. "We could have gotten drunk at home, and Avel might have seen out the evening without getting backhanded."

"No guarantees, even then," Sasha says.

"You boys need me to lay on a car to get you home?" Liza asks.

I nod. "Thank you. You gonna be there tomorrow?"

She shakes her head. "Work is work. But you'd better believe I'm dying to meet the ravishing beauty tying down the elusive and gorgeous Vladimir Kislev!"

∼

Ruined Beauty

Avel falls asleep in the limousine, waking when we drag him into the house. He's arguing with Sasha over whether to order pizza as I sneak away.

I open the door to the bedroom. Morgana is asleep, boxes and bags everywhere, so I assume someone delivered her shopping earlier in the evening. My wedding suit is hanging on a rail in the dressing room, pressed and ready, my shoes shined to perfection on the floor beneath it.

I open a closet, pushing a panel in the back wall. It slides away to reveal a secret compartment.

Mama was spirited away from her Tuscan home to marry my father, but she already had a young man she adored. He wrote her many letters when she still lived in Italy—heartfelt missives proclaiming his love. They had only shared kisses when she had to leave her home, with no time to explain. Mama told my father in a fit of helpless anger, and he swore he would have her lover tracked down and murdered if she spoke his name again.

My father brutally stole Mama's tender virginity, saved for the sweet boy she had dreamed of marrying. She locked her broken heart away right here, and when I was a child, she shared it with me.

I reach into the void and extract the bundle of letters. The one on top is the last one Mama received. My Italian is pretty good, but I don't need to be fluent to read this letter. I know it word for word already.

My beautiful Stefania,

I dream of the day courage finds us, and we tell your father about our love. I will be at your side always, no matter what obstacles stand in our way.

Without your heart to warm me, the world would be as cold as the distant stars. I thank the heavens and the angels for lighting my path and blessing my life.

I can't help falling in love with you.

Love always, Your Luca

I fold the letter carefully and put it back in the bundle. Delving into the secret compartment again, I find the velvet box containing my mother's wedding ring. The one given to my father by Mama's family as a sign of good faith.

It would be laughable if it wasn't so soulless. Luca should have been the one to put that ring on Mama's finger, but her family didn't value her beyond her usefulness as a bargaining chip. That brutal marriage sealed a truce that has stood ever since, keeping our two families in a stand-off. Mutually assured destruction if either side starts a fight.

I close my fist around the ring, warming the gold. My Papa thinks it's in Mama's urn with her ashes. If he finds out I kept it, he'll go fucking crazy.

Mama believed I had love in my heart—she put it there. But she took her love away when she left me, and the pain seared my emotions, leaving me numb. My father beat me for years, but I felt more agony at that moment when Mama's eyes closed for the last time.

I want to go to Morgana and lose myself in her soft curves. But I *don't* want to use her body just to distract myself. Putting my hands on her isn't fair when my head and heart are a million miles away.

I'm just drunk and maudlin, dwelling on the past.

Snap out of it. What's done is done.

24

Morgana

I expected Vlad to return, climb into bed beside me, and fill the house with my screams of ecstasy. I showered, shaved, and did all the gonna-get-laid prep work, only to fall asleep waiting for him.

There's no getting away from it. I want to feel him inside me, even only once. He wants me, too, and nothing is stopping us.

A cramping sensation seizes my stomach. What if he stayed out all night?

No. His blanket is on the couch, and his suit and shoes are gone.

There's a knock on the door. It's Dulcie, carrying a tray, and behind her is a sleepy-looking Lilyana.

"Hi," Lili says. "Dulcie made *sharlotka* and coffee if you'd like it." She catches my confused expression and smiles. "It's

Russian-style apple cake, the best in the world." She thrusts a gift-wrapped parcel into my arms. "And this is for you, from Vladi."

I sit on the couch and undo the silver ribbon. Under the velvet wrapping paper is a box containing something I never thought I'd own.

"Are you crying?" Dulcie asks incredulously. "It's only a camera."

"Only a camera? It's wonderful. The best thing I ever had." I hold the box aloft like it's the Holy Grail. "The Canon EOS R5 is perfect for the pictures I want to take. It has a lag-free viewfinder and top-speed autofocus, including eye and face detection..." my voice tails off as I realize both women are staring at me. "Okay. It's interesting to *me*. I've never even seen a five-thousand-dollar camera before. Vlad can afford anything, but he got me something he knew I would love."

An envelope is taped to the box. Inside is a postcard with a watercolor print of a fox in a snowy forest. He didn't write anything on it, but it makes me smile.

"We'll leave you to it," Dulcie says. "The boys have left, and when Sergey's wheelchair has been prepared, David will take him to the church. I'll help Lilyana get dressed, and when she's ready, I'll send her to you."

"Josie will be here soon. Will you please send her up too?"

"Of course."

I rummage until I find what I need, and I take only a short time to blow-dry and set my hair in rollers. I'm enjoying a piece of the cake when Josie bustles in, buckling under the weight of two garment bags.

"Jesus," she says. "This house is insane. I see the appeal of this bratva lifestyle. Even if Vlad wasn't gorgeous, it'd be worth it." She pours the coffee. "How are you feeling?"

I explain what happened last night. Josie's expression remains neutral, but I know her better than that.

"So you and Vlad are fighting your desire to screw each other senseless, but it looks like you're gonna lose?" She furrows her brow. "Well, maybe you need to get it out of your system. Because actually falling for him would be extremely dumb. He's a killer, Morgana. Is it sensible to mess with the heart of a man who could make you disappear on a whim?"

"*None* of this is sensible," I reply, "but I'm in the thick of it now. There's no backing out, no alternatives. And I can't help how he makes me feel."

Josie spoons sugar into her cup. "And what does *he* think?"

That question gives me pause.

"I think something about me is troubling him. Either he likes me too much, or he's just confused, but he's not handling this supposedly sham relationship with the cold distance I was expecting."

"The stunt you're gonna pull today might clarify matters," Josie says. "He may murder you for your impudence once you've signed the marriage license. He should have booked a funeral straight after and saved paying twice for catering."

Josie unzips the heavier of the two garment bags, and I sigh at the sight of the dress. It's the most beautiful thing I've ever seen and worlds away from the decoy I picked at the boutique.

"The fifth place I called had it in stock." Josie fluffs the skirt. "With it being a corset, it should fit, but we'd better get you into it and see?"

Josie helps me into the dress, lacing the ribbon in the back. The underskirt lifts the layers perfectly, and the kitten heels I chose yesterday set it off to perfection.

I had almost talked myself out of wearing it. But now I see the full effect. There's no way I'm backing out.

Vlad keeps blowing hot and cold, and I'm sick of it. I will defy him today and find out what kind of man he is.

"You look phenomenal," Josie says. "I need to take a photo."

"Use my new camera. It's on the table."

"Vladi got this for you?" Josie unboxes the camera and powers it on. "I think it's gonna be okay, Morgana. I really do. He cares about the things you care about. I bet he won't hurt you or your parents."

"So I should just run away?"

Josie tilts her head. "Is it worth the risk? And do you really want to?"

"No, and no comment, in that order. Help me with my hair?"

~

We're outside the church, and I'm drenched in nerves. I'm surprised at how emotional I feel, given this is all for show.

Lilyana is inside, letting everyone know we're here. I hear a string quartet play 'Canon in D.' Lili reappears, propping the door open.

My father is behind her, carrying a bouquet. He gives the flowers to Lili and smiles broadly, taking my hands in his.

"Dad!" I blink rapidly, trying to stave off tears. "I wasn't expecting you. Why are you here?"

"Mr. Kislev called me early this morning." Dad puts his hand on my cheek. "He has cleared our rent arrears and put five million dollars into our account to apologize for his rudeness in taking you away the way he did. He said he would not ask for my blessing but hoped I would agree to give you away at the ceremony."

What the hell?

"At first, I thought he was being cruel, mocking me," my father continues. "He stole you, after all. But it was the *way* he asked. I said I would attend, but it would be your decision."

"This is crazy. I'm so happy to see you. But who's looking after Mom?"

"Would you believe me if I told you she's here?" Dad's eyes are filling too. "After he took you away, I had to tell her the truth, and she wore herself out screaming at me and crying for hours. But then we received a package full of the best medicine. Treatments we could never afford. Your mother started feeling better almost immediately. She has a way to go, but the light is returning to her eyes." His voice cracks. "I got her back, Morgana. *We* got her back."

I can't believe Vlad did this. He never said a word to me about it. All he did was ask me to wear a specific dress style, and I went behind his back to show my dissatisfaction at his request.

I was worried about the consequences, but now I'm seized by a worse fear that I didn't expect—that I might genuinely hurt him. Am I capable of wounding the heart of the man who kidnapped me and forced me to be his bride?

"Come on, Lili, we're going first," Josie says.

Liliyana hands me the bouquet. "I'm super scared to be in front of all those people," she says."

"You don't have to do anything. I'm just glad you wanted to be here with me. If you're struggling, stand by Vladi and don't look at your father."

Josie takes Lili's hand. "I'll keep hold of you, honey. Just smile and keep putting one foot in front of the other. It's your big brother's wedding day!"

With that, Lili beams. "I love him so much. I can do this."

I stay out of sight, watching my bridesmaids enter the church. My father takes my arm.

"Ready?"

I nod. "Let's go."

25

Vlad

My father sits in the front pew. I haven't spoken to him yet today—I don't want his poisonous words rolling around in my mind.

I'm grateful to have my brothers at my side. Sasha nudges me, and I turn to see Lilyana and Josie gliding gracefully down the aisle.

"Bellissimi angeli," Sasha murmurs. He rarely speaks Italian, so the sight must have moved him.

Lili lets go of Josie's hand and stops walking, her shoulders shaking as she freezes. Josie reaches for her, but she won't move, and a ripple of disquiet moves through the congregation.

My father glares at Lili, but I dare not look at him. I will break his jaw here and now if I see that mocking look of hatred on his sick old face. Instead, I descend the altar steps and go to my sister, taking her hand gently.

"It's okay. Come, be here with us."

Lili falls into step beside me, clinging to my arm. I put her between Arman and Avel, and her twin puts his arm around her shoulder.

"Hush now, Lili," Avel says. "You're alright." He flashes me a grin and winces as the movement stretches his injured lip.

A collective gasp fills the church, and I see Morgana arm in arm with her father.

She isn't wearing the dress she brought home from the boutique.

This gown is everything I told her *not* to wear. Deeply décolleté, with a beaded bodice and the slimmest of shoulder straps, kicking into floaty layers of tulle. The veil is more of a cape, embellished with more beading that matches the dress. Her hair is piled on her head, an emerald comb holding it in place. But none of that is why my father's friends are having conniptions.

Morgana's gown is black. Deep, true ebony, shimmering with pearls of jet and smoky Swarovski crystals.

My gaze settles on her face, seeking the defiance that fuelled her decision to trick me. But all I see is concern. Her eyes shimmer, and her smile isn't genuine.

She looks stunning, but something is bothering her. Has her bravado deserted her? Is she afraid of my reaction?

They reach the altar, and George sits beside David. I turn to face Morgana, my expression stony. The music is still playing.

"Are you angry?" she asks, drawing nearer so she can lower her voice. "I didn't know what you'd done for my parents or that you'd invite them today. You said nothing about that wonderful camera, either. If I'd thought for a second—"

"You're testing my patience, *lisichka*."

Morgana bites her lip, and I feel a rush of pleasure. It's almost a shame to put her out of her misery, but I can't bear to let her suffer for too long.

"God help me." I take her hand. "You look fucking incredible. I'm the luckiest bastard alive."

She flushes with relief, giving me a broad smile. The music fades, and the priest takes his position before us.

"I never promised to be obedient," Morgana whispers.

I squeeze her fingers. "Oh yeah? Well, you're *about* to promise exactly that. It's in the vows. And you won't get off the hook this easily next time."

The priest does his bit, and we do ours. We promise to love, honor, obey, cherish, and protect one another, come what may. Unsurprisingly, it feels hollow, but not because it's fake. It's because I wish it was *real*, and that's a punch to the gut I didn't expect.

The nondescript wedding rings I bought yesterday are in Sasha's pocket, and when the time comes, he hands them to us. Morgana slides my ring onto my finger.

I wish I'd brought Mama's wedding ring with me. Maybe I knew deep down that I'd feel this way and didn't want to risk making a rash decision. As it is, I have no choice, and I push the standard diamond band past Morgana's knuckle without looking at her.

"I now pronounce you man and wife," the priest says. "You may kiss your bride."

My eyes meet Morgana's for the first time since the ceremony began. They sparkle in the candlelight.

Fuck. I've been so caught up in my bullshit that I never stopped to think how she might be feeling. What an asshole I am.

I put a hand on her waist and pull her close. The sudden movement startles her, and she loses her footing, placing her palms on my chest as she stumbles. My other hand slides to the back of her neck, and I breathe in her perfume as our lips meet.

I don't want everyone to see what she does to me, but I can't kiss her and make it look like nothing. As soon as I find her tongue, I'm lost in the moment, pushing my fingers into the hair at her nape. Her warm mouth flexes against mine, her lips supple, and she moves her hand to rest her fingertips on my jawline.

Sasha coughs and kicks my ankle, and reluctantly, I break the kiss. Someone at the back of the church yells, "*nikakogo seksa v tserkvi!*" to raucous laughter. The strings start again, playing a traditional Russian folk song, and people get to their feet, dancing in the aisle.

Morgana frowns at me. "What did he say?"

I grin. "He said, 'no sex in church.' Seems a damn shame. I like the idea of giving The Almighty a show."

"Hell doesn't scare you?"

"I already know that's where I'll end up. At this stage, it's go big or go home."

Morgana wriggles out of my grasp. "So let's attend our reception and play nice. I'm sure you'll have other opportunities to prove you're an abomination before God and man."

"An abomination?" I follow her, dodging flying flower petals and rice. "I thought you didn't like me."

"You did your best to convince me *not* to look past your bullshit." I open the wedding car door, and she dives in, with me behind her. "But you're not what you sell yourself as, are you? You made sure my Mom had her medication. Got my parents here today. Why didn't you tell me you were doing those things?"

"Honestly?" I gather her skirt, trying to pull it into the car so I can shut the door, and she giggles. "I thought you'd run out on me, on the wedding, if you realized I wasn't gonna hurt your parents after all. It wasn't in my interest to lose my leverage."

Morgana waves at her parents as we pull away. "I am sorry about the dress. But your stupid rules got my back up. I thought you were an irredeemable asshole."

"Understandable." I narrow my eyes. "But don't imagine you've got away with it, *lisichka*. I'll get you back for that little performance."

26

Morgana

The terrace looks pretty decorated with string lights. Dulcie barks orders at servers as they rush around with hor d'oeuvres, and at the far side of the rooftop, the bar is serving expertly mixed cocktails.

I'm helping myself to blinis and caviar when the music fades. I look around, wondering what's happening.

Lilyana sits at a white baby grand on a small stage on the terrace, avoiding making eye contact with anyone. Amazing that these things just happen, but this is what it means to be obscenely wealthy.

Vlad appears beside me and takes the plate from my hand.

"It's time," he says. "David will announce us. Just as we rehearsed—basic steps, no lifts or dips."

"Just as well," I reply. "I doubt I could salsa in this dress, anyway."

"Ladies and gentlemen, the bride and groom," David says. He leads the applause, and Vlad and I take the floor.

Lilyana flexes her fingers, and a hush descends on the crowd as she plays. Vlad takes my hand in his, the other at my waist, moving me with more confidence than last night. All around us, strangers' faces soften as they drink in the romance.

And romantic it is. It should feel like a sick mockery, a desecration of something soulful and authentic. But with Vlad's hands on me, I feel truly held. Not just physically, but in my heart.

Is *this* the real him?

Vlad and I are almost cheek-to-cheek. He whispers in my ear.

"Wise men say..."

Tears spring to my eyes.

I'm caught in my feelings, clinging to this man I barely know and cursing my stupid heart. It was bad enough in the church. I hate myself for wishing this beautiful moment wasn't fake, too.

Why must he torment me so?

"Only fools rush in...."

"Don't do this to me," I say, my voice breaking.

Vlad's lips brush my earlobe. "But I can't help..."

I hold my breath, but he doesn't complete the lyrics.

I'm falling for him. Too hard, too fast, but I'm powerless to stop it. Just like the song says, I'm a fool. I'm well on the way to loving this complicated, dangerous man. His arms already feel like home.

Vlad is looking at something behind me, and as we turn, I realize it's Sergey. The old man's expression is pure venom as we spin past him.

Vlad's father sees something, just as Lili does. But if Sergey looks for beauty, it's not so he can appreciate it. If he had his way, he would snuff out our burgeoning feelings for no reason other than malice.

I cling to my husband and wonder what's to become of us. I thought love came *before* heartbreak, but the way I feel now, I'm not sure. We already know we will walk away from one another. Whatever this is will end before it begins.

The song is over, but Vlad holds onto me. Dulcie is handing out shots of vodka to every guest.

"No," Sergey says, still glaring at us. "David, *nyet*. I don't wanna see it."

David waves his hand dismissively. "Oh, shut up, Sergey. It's happening."

"See what?" I frown at Vlad. "What does he mean?"

Vlad wraps his arms around me, pulling me closer. "Someone will take the first shot and shout *'gorko.'* This means the vodka is bitter. We have to kiss for as long as it takes for everyone to drink." He grins. "The sweetness of our union is supposed to take the foul taste away."

"Wow. Has the vodka ever turned to cyanide?"

He laughs. "Bratva couples rarely marry for love. This tradition is a sick joke."

"*Gorko!*" someone yells. Guests knock back their shots, adding more and more voices to the chorus.

"*Gorko! Gorko! Gorko!*"

Vlad smiles at me. "Gotta play to the gallery, *lisichka*."

He takes my face in his hands. If he feels the tears on my cheeks, he doesn't show it. He lowers his lips to mine and kisses me tenderly, to whistles and hollers from the crowd.

∼

I sit with Mom and Dad, watching the party. Now and then, someone stops and says how happy they are for us. I smile graciously and make the right noises. What else can I do?

Mom is nursing a small glass of Chablis. I haven't seen her drink her favorite wine in years, and I can't remember when she last seemed so alive, either.

Vlad is shaking hands with his guests and sharing jokes. He takes the hand of a middle-aged woman, kissing it, and she gives a tinkling laugh.

"That man is a goner for you," Mom says, nodding at my new husband.

"He already told me he doesn't do love." I pick the olive out of my Martini. "Vlad is a red-blooded man. He knows what he wants, but that's no foundation for a marriage. When his father dies, I'll be free and a millionaire."

We fall silent. I watch Vlad smile as Sasha hands him a drink.

"Oh, Morgana," Mom says, putting her hand over mine. "I know you went through a lot of bad stuff with Jack. But he never looked at you like Vlad does." She lowers her voice. "If you put more effort into making it work rather than fighting it, things might end differently. Or not end at all."

"Mom, he's bratva. He's done terrible things and doesn't feel a scrap of remorse. *Should* I love a man like that?"

Mom glances at my dad. He's tucking into canapés and paying no mind to our conversation.

"Your father was a hellion in his younger days." She sips her wine. "And he was a tough nut to crack, too. But let me tell you this, Morgana. If a wicked man grows a heart for you, that's it. You own him. The love of a villain is hard to come by, but it's for keeps."

I'm not in control here, Morgana. No fucking way. That's what Vlad said.

My husband is now standing alone, leaning on the glass wall of the conservatory. He catches my eye but doesn't smile, shifting his gaze into the distance. I knock back the Martini, warmth flooding my senses, and go to him.

Vlad can break the mold. He can be the man he needs to be. The man I *want*. He just has to believe it, too.

27

Vlad

A man is standing a few feet away, holding court with a couple of his cronies. He hasn't noticed I'm watching him.

I know the guy. A banker called Lewis something. He used to be on the board at one of our companies, but his shady dealings came to the attention of the police, so we fired him. He got off the fraud charges, but it cost him plenty, and we contributed to the bill to apologize for shunning him in public.

His friend is talking to him, but he's not paying attention. Instead, his eyes keep sliding across the terrace and settling on my wife's body.

I knock back my drink, keeping hold of the glass, but before I can make a move, Morgana appears in front of me.

"You are standing alone at your wedding reception, looking like you're waiting for a root canal appointment. What's the matter, husband?"

Over her shoulder, I see Lewis nod at Morgana's ass. He leans to say something in his friend's ear, and they both break into sneering grins.

"That fucker over there has a death wish," I say, keeping my voice low. "Excuse me, *lisichka*. I have to make a scene."

Lewis clocks me before I reach him. He throws his hands in the air, spilling his drink on his jacket.

"Vladimir! I was just saying how beautiful she—"

I grab his lapel and knee him firmly in the gut, making him stumble backward. He drops his drink as the balcony rail presses against his lower back. I smash the rim of my glass against the railing, holding the jagged edge to Lewis's cheek. Everyone has fallen silent and is staring at me, but I don't give a shit.

"You mean my wife? My fucking *wife*? How dare you move your eyes over what's mine, you disrespectful piece of—"

"Vladi." I glance around to see Morgana shaking her head. "Stop."

I fling the glass to the ground. Lewis is still frozen in shock, and I set him back on his feet.

The man is drunk, stupid, or both. He belches and speaks again as I turn away.

"Taking orders from some piece of pussy," he says under his breath. "How the mighty have fallen."

A red mist descends in my mind. My eyes meet Morgana's, and I know she heard what he said.

I spin around and deliver a forceful kick to Lewis's stomach, sending him toppling off the balcony. "Who's fucking falling now?" I shout after him.

Lewis screams as he smashes into David's Mercedes, fucking it up entirely. A quick glance confirms the mouthy bastard is dead.

My father is sitting nearby in his wheelchair. He laughs so hard that Dulcie has to run and help him with his oxygen mask. Morgana turns away from me, returning to her shocked parents, and David claps his hands to get everyone's attention.

"Okay, nothing to see here," he says. "Let's get on with our evening."

The music restarts, and the hubbub of conversation rises. David approaches me, putting his hand on my shoulder.

"Lewis planned to run for Congress next year, and the man owed us big. So congratulations on ruining my car *and* your bratva's chance to put a puppet in Washington."

I scowl. "I don't fucking care, David. Leave me alone. I did what Papa asked of me and got married against my will. Isn't it enough?"

I give David my back and almost walk straight into my wife.

"My parents are leaving," she says. "It's too much for them. Being married to you is gonna be this way, isn't it? You'll dance with me and break my heart with your kisses, yet kill in cold blood anyone who shows me a modicum of disrespect?"

I'm trying to listen to her, but Dulcie is waving at me to get my attention.

"Yes. No one offends you and lives." I meet her eyes. "I'm sorry. You're right. The codicil in Papa's will is now in effect, and when he dies, I'll be sworn in as Pakhan. Then, if you choose to leave, I won't stop you." I take her hand and bring it to my lips, kissing her palm. "I could *make* you stay, but I won't. Perhaps you'll consider remaining by my side when the time comes."

In my peripheral vision, I see Dulcie beckoning me urgently. *What the fuck is wrong now?*

"Gotta deal with something," I say to Morgana. "Hang out with Josie. Enjoy yourself."

"She left. She thought Sasha was ignoring her, so she drank too much and ducked out early. I don't mind, though. I'm gonna go to bed." A question hesitates on her lips before rushing out. "Do you expect to join me there tonight?"

"Expect?" I release her hand. "No. But I dare to hope."

My wife grants me a wry smile before she walks away.

I dodge through the guests, catching Dulcie near the elevator. She grips my arm.

"Your father isn't doing so well, Vladi. He wants to see you immediately."

Papa's breathing comes in harsh rasps. He's sitting in the chair beside his bed, his oxygen mask in his hand.

"You should use that," I say as I walk in. "Or not. It won't make much difference in the end."

He scowls. "Big, bad Vlad. Except you're not, are you? I saw how you looked at that girl when she walked toward you in the church. How you kissed her. And now poor Lewis is being scraped off the sidewalk, and for *what*? I taught you better than that."

"Don't bring Morgana into it." I sit on the edge of the bed. "I got married, and you got what you fucking wanted."

"No, I didn't." Papa coughs into his elbow, and I see blood on his sleeve. "I did what was necessary to ensure my oldest son was strong enough to lead. *Now* look at you. Do you think loving your wife will make you better than me? Soft-hearted, you are. Still clinging to memories of your Mama's coddling like a little boy."

"I've heard it all before, Papa. What do you have left to threaten me with? The marriage is official, and I met your will conditions."

"David will be your second," Papa says. "Not Sasha or Avel or anyone else. And he will more than likely try to take the bratva from you. Can you stop him?"

"You bastard. You couldn't resist fucking with us all from beyond the grave. Why didn't you just hand the bratva to David in the first place and spare me all this?"

"Because David didn't pay his dues like you and I did," Papa hisses. "Your grandfather ignored David and put all his energy into me. David must have the courage to *take* what he wants rather than have it handed to him."

Pitting people against each other has always been Papa's strongest suit. For every winner, there must always be a loser.

"You *want* David and I to destroy each other?"

Papa shrugs. "One of you will come out on top. The strongest. The one who deserves to be Pakhan." He grins at me, showing his yellow teeth. "I won't live to see whether your Mama's ways or mine will be the making of you, but you will find out soon enough."

"Everything's a game to you, isn't it?" I get to my feet. "You think you won? Look around. When you die, neither I nor your other children will mourn you as a father. Will your empire lament your death? Does your money love you back? Will the associates and cronies you know so well shed a tear for you? Living without love didn't make you strong, Papa. It made you lonely and bitter, and now you see me choosing differently, you're feeling it. Aren't you?"

Papa closes his eyes. "I chose power and control. My heart is too hardened to know loneliness, so if you're hoping I'll relent and beg your forgiveness, forget it. Don't go looking for my regrets. I have none."

I put my mouth beside his ear. "Everything is *mine*. All the money, the entire empire. You made me suffer my whole life for this bratva's future, so I'll be damned if anyone takes it from me."

I don't know if Papa is listening to me. He seems peaceful now. He knew his passing wouldn't bring grief, so he settled for paranoia and tension instead.

"We will bury you with the respect a pakhan deserves," I say, "but weeds will grow around your headstone. Your velvet portrait will be unhung. And I'll take Mama's wedding ring to the man she truly loved and put it into his hand."

My father's head whips around. He starts to say something but chokes on his words, his chest convulsing as he hacks.

"For myself, my brothers, Lilyana, and Mama, I say this, Sergey Ivanovich Kislev." I smile at his stricken face. "Fuck you."

I leave the room on fast feet, ignoring the bellows of rage behind me. My thoughts are clearer than they've ever been.

I need my wife.

28

Morgana

I sit in my underwear before the mirror and take out my emerald earrings, grateful not to have to bear their weight anymore. You don't realize how heavy real jewels are when you're used to cheap costume junk.

I'm married to a man I met just a couple of days ago. A man who just added to his murder tally. Six are now dead at his hands because of me.

This same man had my mother's medication delivered to her door. He asked my father to attend our wedding and give me away. He loves his brothers and Lilyana most of all. His housekeeper speaks fondly of him and tells me his Mama adored him. And he respects my boundaries, even though we're clearly burning with lust for one another.

I was so sure he was another abusive asshole. All the signs were there. But with Jack and Hektor, kindness and affection were just part of the mask, the facade that hid the rotten, toxic mess behind. With Vlad, it's the other way around—the good stuff he tries so hard to bury is who he really is.

The bratva life hardened him in some ways. Murdering people and not feeling any way about it is definitely not a mainstream skill set. But Vlad's vicious possessiveness turns me on just as much as his soft side, and he saw that in me from the beginning.

I'm falling hard for the monster *and* the man, no matter how hard I try to deny it to myself.

I hear the suite door open. Vlad appears behind me in the mirror. He leans on the doorframe.

"Hello, wife. To be clear, I am not here to banter, bicker, tease or otherwise fuck around. I want you, and this time you'll need to work hard to convince me to back off."

I turn around. "What about the party?"

"Fuck the party, fuck all of it. I'm tired of the expectations, the pantomime, the lies." He takes a step toward me. "You exasperate me, Morgana. You're impudent, audacious, and smart. Everything a bratva wife *shouldn't* be, and everything that ought to drive me up the fucking wall. But I adore you because you're a challenge. Your love doesn't have a dollar value, which makes me want it all the more."

My breath catches, but I get a hold of myself. "So, in that case, shouldn't I keep saying no to you?"

Vlad stares at me for a moment before dropping to his knees.

"You want me to beg, is that it? I've never begged for anything, but if you want me to scrape and plead for permission to touch you, I will. Just don't tell anyone."

I get to my feet, gesturing for him to stand. "You're a pakhan, Vladi. You don't belong on your knees."

"Agreed. But you'd look fucking gorgeous on yours." He raises an eyebrow as he pulls me to him. "What does my wife want? Because *I* wanna make you scream."

I want him to ravage me every which way until I'm sore and spent. And I'm done fighting myself, fighting him. I'd rather regret what I do than what I don't.

"Okay." I wrap my arms around his neck. "Give it your best shot."

Vlad doesn't hesitate. With a growl, he ducks under my arm and puts me over his shoulder, lifting my feet from the ground. I yelp with shock as he carries me into the bedroom, dumping me on my back on the mattress. Then he's on top of me, his lips crushing mine.

My pussy floods instantly. *Dear God.* I thought I'd experienced desire before, but this is something else. A primal, gnawing hunger in my core that's almost painful in its urgency. I want everything all at once—his mouth, his tongue, his hands, his cock.

He straddles me, his breathing harsh. I close my eyes and sigh as he slides his hands over my bare thighs. He shifts to his knees on the floor, his breath warm between my legs, and I shudder.

I'm about to let this murdering bratva brute eat me out, and I don't give a damn. I need release, or I'll go crazy.

"Just do it before I change my mind."

"Bullshit," Vlad says. "Your little pussy is desperate for me."

He slides a fingertip over my soaked panties, pressing insistently on my pussy lips. I moan as he moves, the pressure finding my sensitive little button. He lifts the material at the edge and slips his finger between my soft folds.

"So wet for me. That's what I like. You gonna drown me?"

I can do nothing but whimper as he massages my clit gently, rolling it beneath his fingertip. He pulls my panties aside, plunging his tongue into me, and I arch my back. He places his palm on my abdomen and holds me in place as I writhe.

"You taste so good." He lashes at my clit with his tongue before taking it between his lips, sucking gently. "So fresh and sweet. Are you gonna be a good girl and come on my face?"

I buck my hips, and he laughs. He slips his finger inside me and growls with delight as my pussy squeezes it.

"Do it to me, Vlad. I want it."

"*Want* it?" Vlad adds a second finger, the stretch easing the almost painful need deep inside me. "You'd better fucking *need* it, Morgana. I don't get off on anything less. Now, look at me."

I lean on my elbows and drag my eyes to his. He holds my gaze as he fingers me, his intensity almost as much of a turn-on as what he's doing. He reaches for me, his fingers wrapping around my throat.

"Who do you belong to?" he says, his voice thick with lust.

"You." The word comes as naturally as my breath. "I belong to *you*."

Vlad has no right to make me say that. He's stolen my future, dignity, and freedom. I can't call my body my own, either, but I don't care. If fucking my husband is wrong, I don't want to be right.

My throat burns as Vlad tightens his grip. His fingers are moving rapidly now, driving me toward the edge. My pussy is spasming, trying to draw him deeper, and I cry out as my climax hits.

With that, Vlad shoves me onto my back again, freeing his fingers. He holds my legs open with both hands and pushes his face into my pussy, his lips pulling at my tender clit as I come. Fluid gushes over his face, but he doesn't let up, and I scream as my orgasm deepens, the intense ecstasy giving way to a sensation of warm, molten pleasure deep in my core.

Vlad sits beside me on the bed. "You're gorgeous, *lisichka*," he says, wiping his face with the back of his hand. "And you taste even better than I imagined."

29

Vlad

I can't believe this beautiful woman is my wife.

Morgana is a vision, her lean limbs glistening with perspiration, her breathing still frantic. I've always thought Fate owed me for what it put me through, but she's still better than a man like me deserves.

"You'd better have more to give me," I say.

She rolls onto her front and drops her head onto her arm, gazing at me. "Is this what you're always like?" she asks.

I grin. "You'll have to stay forever to know for sure, won't you?"

She sticks her tongue out at me, and that's all the provocation I need. I stand and strip, laughing at Morgana's slack-jawed stare.

"Oh, Vladi," she sighs. "You're too much, you know."

I grab my cock and work it a little, and her eyes widen. "I think you can handle me," I say. "But you've been seriously teasing me, and I can't promise to take it easy on you."

"Please don't," she says, sliding to the floor. "You gotta give me a minute here, though. Let me distract you."

Her perfect makeup hasn't got a chance in hell.

She smiles sweetly and tilts her head back, closing her eyes. "Do what you imagined doing," she murmurs. "I know you were thinking of me that first night. I came in while you were showering and heard you moaning my name."

Damn. If I'd known she was there, I'd have dragged her in there with me.

I dig my hands into her hair, dragging the pins loose. Her chestnut waves cascade over her shoulders, and I gather the hair in my hand, winding it into a tight rope around my fingers. My cock throbs in my grip, and I rest the swollen head on her lips, rubbing my pre-come into them.

"And what did you think about that, *lisichka*?" I ask.

"I went back to my bed and touched myself," she says. She laps at me with the tip of her tongue, and my knees threaten to buckle. "That's twisted, right?"

"What isn't? You and I are just two more people fucking our lives up. But I wouldn't change a thing."

Morgana opens her mouth and takes me deep into her throat. The sensation steals my breath for a moment, and I give a long groan of satisfaction.

I didn't realize how close I was to losing my mind, but now I have my wife at my feet, I can take on the whole damn world. I'll do whatever it takes to turn the lie into truth and keep her by my side.

I let go of my cock and grab Morgana's head with both hands. My fingers dig into her skull as I square my stance, thrusting into her warm mouth. Her lips yield to me, her throat closing around my shaft, and I feel my climax building deep in my abdomen.

Not yet.

With a growl of frustration, I yank her head back and withdraw from her face, my cock coated in thick saliva. I let go of her hair, grabbing her neck and squeezing it as I jerk my cock.

"Fuck," she gasps. "That's *so* hot."

Her hand is between her legs, moving inside her panties. Knowing she's playing with herself almost sends me over the edge.

"I never said you could do that," I say, hauling her to her feet and slapping her hand away from her pussy. I put my spit-covered palm on her face and smear her already-trashed makeup. "I still need to get you back for your wedding dress stunt."

Still holding her throat, I spin her around and push her onto the bed face down. She squeaks in shock and attempts to roll away, but I'm on her before she can move. I lean on her back to hold her in place as I peel off her panties.

"You dick. What are you gonna do to me?"

"*Lisichka*, it's what I'm *not* gonna do." I sit back on my heels and part her ass cheeks with my hands, tucking my cock between them. "Remember when I said I wouldn't fuck you unless you ask?"

She looks over her shoulder at me, amber eyes smoldering, and nods.

"Well, you're the only person in the world who could reduce me to begging, so I intend to redress the balance." I slide my cock along her valley, teasing her asshole, and she buries her face in the duvet with a moan. "I'm not gonna fuck you until you're as desperate as I am," I swat her ass cheek lightly, "and that's not the only way I can punish you."

Morgana squirms, and I unclasp her bra, dragging it from beneath her and tossing it to the floor. I run my hand between her shoulder blades.

"Vladi, please—"

I raise my hand and bring it crashing down on the soft flesh of her ass. She yelps, trying to prop herself on her hands and push me off.

"Oh my God!" she cries. "You can't do that!"

"Don't you like it?" I ask, kneading her buttock to ease the sting.

"No!"

She pushes back against me, and I slide the tip of my cock over her slick pussy lips. Her wetness feels so good that it's all I can do not to plunge into her, but I resist.

I spank her again, the sound cracking the air. My hand stings from the impact, and Morgana moans as she moves her body against me, trying to get me to enter her.

"You're a fucking terrible liar," I say, nudging inside her a little. "You want me in your little cunt, and you're making no effort to convince me otherwise, so give it up. *Beg* me."

"It's worth it," she gasps, "because I know you're suffering at least as much as I am."

"Still pretending to hate me?" I bring both hands down hard on Morgana's ass before grabbing the cheeks, gripping them as I make tiny movements with my hips. "You don't. You *can't*. Admit it, and I'll give you what you want, now and forever." I tug her hair with one hand, gripping her shoulder and pulling her onto all fours. "What do I want to hear?" I give her a couple more inches. "Come on."

"Oh, fuck. Okay, I don't hate you. I'm begging. Please, Vladi. *Please*. I need you."

I bottom out inside her with one firm thrust, holding her in place so she has to take it. She cries out, her pussy clutching at my cock.

"This is gonna be quick and dirty," I say, clasping my fingers around her neck again, "but you *will* come too. No way my wife settles for one orgasm, not on our wedding night. So work that clit for me like a good girl, and don't keep me waiting."

I pull out of her and plunge back in, hissing through my teeth. She's so *tight*. She's gonna milk the come out of me in no time. I feel her fingertips on her pussy, moving rapidly over her swollen clit as I rail her.

"Tell me when you're coming." I let go of her hair and take hold of her waist so I can fuck her harder. "Make that juicy pussy go crazy for me. I can't hold off much longer. You feel too fucking good."

"I'm coming!" she cries, throwing her head back. "Give me more!"

Her screams are all I need. I pump my hips, slamming her again and again as her wet pussy clutches my cock. Pleasure seizes my body, my energy draining into her as I climax.

I roll off Morgana's prone body and lie on my back, waiting for my breathing to calm. The sounds of the party above filter through the ceiling. I doubt anyone heard us over the hubbub, but I don't give a shit either way.

Morgana rolls onto her side and rests her chin on my shoulder. "You're a cruel man, Vladi. My ass is numb, my throat is sore inside and out, and I'm sure I'll be able to feel you inside me for days."

I smile at her, leaning across to pull the duvet over us. "There are no half-measures with a man like me. And you embarrassed me today, wearing a fucking sexy black dress and flaunting your beautiful body in front of everyone I know. I specifically told you what to wear, and you let me spend—wait." I frown. "How did you even get that dress?"

"Josie put it on her credit card. You owe her for that, by the way."

I shake my head. "You're gonna be a handful, aren't you?"

She drops the duvet, flashing her tits at me. "More than a handful, wouldn't you say? Now I'm gonna run a bath and wash your grime away."

I laugh. She leaves the room, and I close my eyes.

Who must I be to deserve a woman like Morgana? I never believed I could do the love thing, but maybe I *can* be that man and still be a powerful leader. Papa was right—he didn't teach me shit worth knowing. But my Mama sure did, and like my asshole father said, maybe her ways will win the day.

I stood beside Morgana and swore to cherish and protect her. To *love* her. I'll have to work on love, but protection? That I *can* do.

I walk into the ensuite to find her wrapped in a towel and pouring bath oil under the running water. "Morgana, I need to know. Who or what gives you those nightmares?"

She freezes for a second, then pulls the towel tightly around her. "I didn't realize you knew. When did I—"

"That first night." I take her hand. "You were crying out, and before I knew what was happening, you were in my arms. It felt wrong to shrug you off, so I lay beside you and crashed out."

Morgana's eyes shimmer, and without words, I know she understands.

Genuine vulnerability must be earned; now is the right time to ask. I won't drag it out of her or use it to hurt or mock her. Whether she's willing or able to tell me is another matter entirely.

Morgana shuts off the faucet and sits on the bathtub's rim. She draws a deep breath.

"My ex, Jack," she whispers. "He put me through hell."

I want to listen to her, but I'm already running ahead in my mind.

Get a name. Get Arman on it. Find this fucker and destroy everything he cares about, then make him beg to die.

"Jack?" I squeeze Morgana's hand, and she looks at me. "Jack what?"

She sniffs, piqued at my priorities. "That was the name he went by, but his real name was Cassius. Cassius Jackson."

Someone hammers on the suite door, and we both jump. I run out to find Sasha barging in.

"Vladi, Papa's gone. Dulcie went to him and found him not breathing. Come and help me get rid of the guests before they figure out something is wrong."

30

Four hours later...

Morgana

The guests left, and Sergey's doctor arrived to sign the death certificate, the undertaker hot on his heels. Vlad and his brothers silently carried the coffin to the hearse, with David and Arman following behind. No one felt moved to go with their father's body. Lilyana retreated to her room, taking her feelings with her.

Now we're in the downstairs lounge, and the atmosphere is oppressive. The men drink hard, refilling their glasses every few minutes. Vlad stares out the window.

"Arman," he says at last. "I know I said no business today, but I need you to find someone."

Everyone looks at Vlad.

"Who?" Arman asks.

"Cassius Jackson." Vlad turns around, his face shadowed in the low light. "I want the cunt alive, for now."

"Vladi, Sergey isn't even cold!" David says, getting to his feet. "Why should we—"

"*I* am pakhan now," Vlad snaps, "and I won't tolerate dissent. Papa is gone, so do what I fucking say."

Arman raises his hands. "I can find out if anyone knows him. But what about the guy trying to find out who killed Hektor? Which is the priority here?"

My voice trembles as I speak. "Vladi, you never told me about that. Does Hektor have a boss? Is he after you?"

"It's none of your business, Morgana."

"You killed him because he was my pimp, so it *is* my business."

The men stare at me in shock.

"You were a hooker?" Sasha asks.

Vlad socks Sasha in the jaw. The blow catches him off guard, and Vlad swings again, his knuckles connecting with his brother's temple. Sasha raises his knees and kicks Vlad in the chest with both feet.

"Break it up!" Avel cries, leaping in between them. He jabs a finger at Vlad. "You and Sasha have never got into a fistfight before. What the *fuck* are you doing? Our asshole father is dead and gone, but right now, it feels like he's still here."

Vlad looks from Sasha to me and back again. He seems suddenly exhausted.

"Sasha, *never* disrespect my wife again. Do you understand?"

"No, I fucking don't." Sasha stands, flexing his jaw. "You think *I'm* the unstable one?" He points at me. "Morgana was completely innocent of this savage world we live in. You dragged her into it, then went on a happy little murder spree on her behalf with no regard for the consequences. We'd know if Hektor belonged to any of our rivals, so you've picked a fight with someone from out of town. Someone who may be stronger than us. So don't talk to me about your fucking responsibility until *you* learn the meaning of the word."

After a sickeningly tense silence, Vlad leaves the room without a word. The front door opens, then closes again.

I'm afraid.

Vlad's attention dazzled me, but I must accept the harsh reality of being with him. The Kislev wealth is dirty money, every cent, and their lives are steeped in death to a degree I am just beginning to comprehend. Yet as Vlad takes the role he has been preparing for his whole life, he's thinking of *me*, putting my safety before that of his bratva. What does his family think of that?

I can't run to my parents or Josie. I'm Hektor's ex-employee—they could get to him through me or hurt the people I love.

"I'm sorry, Morgana," Sasha says. "Don't worry. He'll be back."

I nod. "Okay. I'll get out of everyone's way."

I jar awake, sitting bolt upright in bed. I don't know what stirred me from sleep, but it's dark, and Vlad isn't beside me. My pillow is still damp from my tears.

I fear for my husband. He hated his father, sure, but that doesn't mean Sergey's death means nothing.

Some say the opposite of love is hate, but there's not much to separate the two. Both involve powerful feelings and obsession. Indifference is the counter-point.

Obligations burden Vlad. To his family, his bratva. And to *me*. Am I just making everything more complicated for him? He just needed a wife so he could inherit his dues, but things weren't going the way he expected. Why does he feel a visceral need to protect me? He doesn't need to make his life more complicated by looking for my ex when he has more significant problems.

A faint sound coming from below. The piano. Why is Lili playing in the middle of the night?

That song again. The song Vlad sang to me as we danced just hours ago. The rhythm is different, a little slower, more halting. I pull on a robe and head downstairs, stopping on the mezzanine above the foyer.

Vlad is at the piano, his back to me. He presses the keys carefully so as not to make them clatter, and the music warms me.

I'm light on my feet as I approach the piano. "So you can play. Why didn't you tell me?"

My husband looks careworn. "I didn't think I'd want to share it with you," he says, still playing. "But things have a way of changing."

He takes his right hand off the keys and reaches it around me, pulling me to sit on his knee. I wrap my arm around his shoulder, and he rests his head on my collarbone. My fingers stroke the fine silver hair above his ear.

"I can read music," he says. "Not as well as Lili, but well enough. I know this song by heart, though. Mama loved it."

He finds the tune, and I tuck myself in so he can reach the keys more easily.

"She taught me when I was very young." Vlad sounds peaceful as he takes solace in the memory. "It was the first piece Lili learned, too, because I taught it to her. When she came home from the hospital, I played it to help her heal. It's what my Mama would have done if she were here."

My heart is breaking at the thought of the younger Vlad, distraught and half-crazy with worry for his little sister, playing the song his mother loved.

"You're good to Lili. Your mother would be proud of how well you care for her."

"No, she wouldn't." Vlad hits a bum note but continues to play. "It's because of me that Lilyana got hurt." He takes his hands off the keys and wraps his arms around me. "My father didn't care to trouble himself with the twins, so I did a ton of babysitting whether or not I wanted to. I was thirty-one and taking care of six of our businesses simultaneously, so I was getting burned out and resentful." He exhales. "We were at our house in the Hamptons, and Papa had fucked off with his cronies. Lili was driving me crazy that day. She was so outgoing back then, so daring, climbing everything."

Vlad's fingers tense on my thigh, and I put my hand over his. I don't know why he's telling me this now, but I won't stop him.

"I needed a minute, so I went outside and down the steps to the deck. Lili thought I was angry with her. I hadn't shut the door properly, and she came running out." He buries his face in my shoulder. "I don't sleep much, but I see three things in my dreams. My father's face as he beat me, Mama's eyes closing for the last time, and Lili," his voice catches, "Lili at the top of those steps, saying 'Vladi, don't be mad.'"

My eyes spill over.

"She tripped and fell the whole way. Although I did what I needed to and got an ambulance, I lost my shit and couldn't stop crying. Papa told me to stop being a pussy. He punched me for the first time since I was a teenager, but I remember little else. I sat beside her in the hospital day and night."

"It was an accident," I say. Vlad's cheek is wet under my palm. "These things happen."

Vlad ignores my remark. "My family is relying on me. David thinks I'm not good leadership material, and he may want to take control of the bratva. It may be Papa's mind games that got me thinking that way. But killing Hektor *will* have consequences. I just don't know what they'll be."

"If it weren't for me, you wouldn't have this problem. Please get the people I love to safety. They may be in danger."

"Okay." Vlad nudges me to my feet. "We're not going on honeymoon anyway, not with a funeral to arrange. I'll give your parents our tickets."

"Thank you." I furrow my brow. "Where were we going?"

"Italy. Tuscan country villa, calm and peaceful. I'll make travel arrangements for you and Josie, too."

I shake my head. "I can't leave. I'd go insane from worry. You're gonna deal with this new enemy *and* go after Jack."

"Don't call him that," Vlad says. "His name is Cassius, not whatever pet name you had for him." The anger drains from his voice. "My life will always be this way. If you stay with me, you'll forever be looking over your shoulder."

He's right. Unless his prosperous bratva collapses around him because of me.

"*If* I left now," I ask, "would you drop it? Would you forget about Cassius? Apologize to Hektor's boss, pay him, try to avoid a war?"

"No." Vlad doesn't smile. "You could spit in my face and storm out right now, and it'd change nothing. I'll take the fight to Hektor's boss and force him to back off." His face darkens. "And as for Cassius, he's dead. He'll rue the day he set eyes on you, Morgana. You have my word. Fight me, hate me, leave me, but I'll still destroy anyone who dares to hurt you. I failed to keep Lili safe and won't make the same mistake again."

I take his hands in mine. "You're not the man I believed you to be. I don't know whether I'm falling for you or going crazy, but I don't wanna be alone tonight."

Vlad stands, and I'm in his arms, my head on his chest. His heart beats against my ear.

"Take me to bed," I whisper. "I need you."

31

Vlad

I thought I'd be glad when my father died. I thought seeing his body would make my cold heart sing with joy. But I just feel numb.

My father's approval was the only thing I wanted as a kid. The more he beat me, the more he screamed in my face, the more I craved a kind word. It would have meant everything if he'd told me he was proud of me. Just *once*.

I had Mama, and she tried to soothe me with her gentle love. But she and my father were like two sides of the same coin, and the more fiercely she loved me, the more Papa battled to tear me and her to pieces.

Now my father is gone, and I have what I want. The bratva is mine, the businesses too. All the money, the assets, everything. But now, at the pinnacle of my life's purpose and the realization of my destiny, I see how utterly fucking pointless it is.

I expected to be partying in the hours following my father's passing. Drinking, raising hell, living it up, knowing the vicious piece of shit couldn't get to me anymore. But I'm at the piano for the first time since Lili's accident, picking out the song Mama would have sung to her baby twins if she'd lived. And my wife—the woman I married purely to serve my selfish purposes—is here with me. Accepting the broken parts of me without question, without mocking.

I couldn't have predicted needing her this way. But with her here on my knee, cradling my head, I can imagine a brighter future. One with her in it, if she'll have me.

I take Morgana's hand without a word and lead her upstairs. As soon as the door of our suite closes behind us, I'm upon her, holding her head in both hands as I drop urgent kisses on her lips.

"You need *me*?" I say between kisses. "*Lisichka*, you don't know the meaning of the word. If I don't feel your skin on mine soon, I'll lose my fucking mind."

Morgana reaches beneath my shirt, sliding her palm over my chest. Her other hand grabs my belt, pulling my hips toward her.

"Do what you gotta do, Vladi. I'm here for you."

She knows I'm all fucked up tonight, but for whatever reason, she's choosing to trust me. It feels damn good.

"Do something for me." I cup her ass, molding her body to mine. "I need to let all this tension go, and I don't wanna hurt you doing it. You like being my good girl, right?"

Morgana's mouth falls open. She nods.

"So edge the hell out of me." I move toward the bedroom, taking her with me. "Get me wound up tight until I'm feral, then fuck it out of me. I'm a big boy. I'll use my words and tell you how it feels."

We fall flat onto the bed, her on top. She shucks off her robe, treating me to the sight of her cream satin nightgown.

"Wedding night lingerie," she says, kissing me.

"Fucking hell. Is it still our wedding night?" I grip her buttocks with both hands, and she giggles. "I'm all over the place."

"You really want me to tease you?"

"Yes. In fact, to hell with it." I roll her off me and stand, going to the closet. "Tie me down and do it."

She frowns. "I could just kill you and run."

I grab two neckties from the rack and throw them on the bed. "Absolutely. And at this stage, I don't give a shit as long as you fuck me first."

I'm only half-joking. It's not that I think she'll hurt me—it's how little I care about the risk. I want to trust my wife, and if she doesn't murder me and flee *now*, she never will.

I assume the classic on-the-back position, and Morgana lashes my hands to the bedposts, doing a pretty good job. Could I break these bonds if I had to? Maybe. But I sure as hell wouldn't bet on it.

"I never tied anyone up before. You look so hot, Vladi. My badass bratva husband, at my mercy."

"Just don't make me regret it." She straddles my thighs. "I wanna suffer for you, *lisichka*. I've made *you* suffer for me. It's only fair."

Morgana unbuttons my shirt, baring my chest. "I'm gonna have so much fun working out what lights you up." She pinches my nipple firmly. "Have you done anything like this before? I haven't."

"Nuh-uh. In fact," my voice trails off as she moves her tongue along the tendon in my neck, "I haven't spent long enough with any woman for her to learn my body. I told you—I have few liaisons."

"*Had*. That's in the past now. I have you, and you have me."

She grazes my nipple with her teeth, and I arch my back. *Fuck*, that feels good. Who knew?

I strain against my bonds, my cock swelling as my wife's weight shifts. Part of me regrets telling her to tease me, but that part is always in a fucking hurry. I want to lose myself in her, and that's what I will do.

Morgana makes short work of the rest of my clothes. I don't like to be vain, but I don't work out just for something to do, and it gives me great pleasure to see her eyes glaze with lust.

"I'm not sure I'll ever get used to seeing you naked, Vladi." She traces her fingertip from my balls to my swollen tip, and I moan. "And I'm so excited to play with this."

"Please do." I jerk my hips. "Because it's so hard, it hurts. Be good and take pity on me."

In a fluid motion, she throws her nightgown over her head and is naked too. It's the first time I've gotten a good look at her body, and the sight does nothing to calm my raging erection.

"Jesus Christ." I drop my head back onto the pillow as she takes my cock in her hand, gripping it at the base. "I've never wanted anyone like I want you. From the moment I met you, I was fucking gone."

Morgana laps at the sweet spot on the underside of the head. I clench my fists and moan through gritted teeth.

"That's it. Fuck, you're a good girl. My good girl. Do that again."

I swear I'm seeing stars. She's reducing all the desire, energy, and tension to that tiny area, and it's bliss.

"Do you want a little more?" she asks.

"Abso-fucking-lutely. Look at me." She gives me her honey-colored eyes. "Take me in your mouth, good and deep. Right into your throat. I wanna feel my wife choking on my cock."

She opens up wide, and I watch my length disappear. The muscles in her throat flex against me, closing as she hits her limit. She coughs and pulls back, thick saliva glistening all over my shaft.

"You're so pretty, Morgana. Look how well you take me. You're doing such a good job." I smile at her. "I never knew my wife would be such a slut for my dick."

She smirks and slaps my cock, making me cry out. "How rude. I can keep doing this all night, you know."

"No way. I'd break these ties and fuck you even if I had to fracture my wrist to do it."

Morgana laughs as she pumps my cock. The saliva provides excellent lubrication, and the friction is just right.

"Don't make me come yet, Morgana. I don't want this to end."

"So, what *do* you want?" She slows her movements. "Or do you want me to decide?"

"Seeing as you're such a good girl, I'll leave it up to you," I say. "But I wanna finish inside you."

The mattress bounces beneath her as she stands astride my chest, showing off. Her pussy is shaved smooth except for a cute little landing strip. She faces my feet and gets on all fours, opening herself up and giving me a magnificent view of her pink lips.

"So I'm gonna play with you and myself while I'm at it. You can't do anything but watch."

Me and my fucking stupid ideas. I never knew she'd be so good at this.

"That's cruel." I flex my wrists. "You're not gonna let me tongue that tight pussy of yours?"

"Maybe a bit." I shudder as she runs the flat of her tongue over my balls. "But I'll ride you when I'm ready. If that's acceptable to you, husband?"

"Yes." I pump my hips, slapping my cock on her cheek. "Of course it's fucking acceptable. Now get on with it. I can only sacrifice so much blood before I pass out."

Morgana wraps her lips around the swollen head and takes me deep again. I push my feet into the mattress and thrust my hips upward, trying to fuck her face. She nips my inner thigh.

"Goddammit!" My eyes roll as she deep-throats me. "That's so fucking incredible. You're so good at this, taking me all the way down."

Morgana's hand appears between her thighs. She opens up her pussy lips with her fingers, exposing the deep rosy flesh of her depths. Her clit looks delicious, and I moan with longing as she strokes it.

"I wanna eat you. Let me have a taste, *lisichka*. Give me just a little."

She doesn't speak with her mouth full, but she hums her disagreement, the vibration sending waves of pleasure through me. The sight of her fingertips massaging her tender little button is incredible, her pussy growing wetter as I watch. I'm gonna slide inside her so easily, and it's gonna have to be soon because I'm developing a problem.

"Morgana, I'm getting close. You're sucking me so well, and I can't take any more. Ride me until I fill that tight little hole with my come."

32

Morgana

Sergey is dead. Vlad won.

But I knew the battle was just beginning when I saw him at the piano. To accept the person he truly is, he has to reject his father's shitty take on life and forge a new path for himself.

I could leave. I *should*. But not now. Vlad needs relief in every sense of the word.

I release him from my mouth and sit back on my heels, my pussy on his face. He spears me with his tongue. The sensation is incredible, but it's not enough, and I squeeze his tongue with my inner walls, trying to feel more.

Am I so turned on that I'm tormenting myself as much as him? His praise is doing it for me in a big way. I never knew I would love being a good girl so much.

Reluctantly, I lift myself off him, sliding down his body reverse-cowgirl-style until his cock is nestled against my inner thigh. My wetness mingles with his as I move my hips back and forth, rubbing him over my pussy.

Fuck, he's big. Riding him like this is gonna be a hell of a workout. Beats spin class any day.

"Morgana." Vlad's voice is stern but with an edge of desperation. "I didn't know what I was asking for. I'm losing my mind here. Stop it."

"You haven't gone feral yet," I say.

I glance over my shoulder at him, and I'm shocked. He's breathing heavily, his skin shimmering with perspiration. The veins and tendons of his arms stand out as he tenses against his bindings, and his stormy eyes hold mine as he speaks.

"Get on my cock *now*."

"No." I grab his erection and rub the head over my clit. "I might just use you to make *myself* come, and then we'll see."

With a roar, Vlad slings his hips firmly, almost throwing me off. I fall backward onto his chest, my head beside his, and he bites my throat.

"Ow!"

"Fucking feral enough for you?" He yanks his arms in toward his body, and the bedposts make a cracking sound. "Release me now, or I'll break both arms to get to you."

I reach and untie one of his hands.

"Don't you fucking move," he says, his lips beside my ear. He unpicks the knot on the other tie in seconds, then wraps both arms around me so I can't escape. I'm on my back on top of him, his body hot and alive beneath me. His cock is huge between my thighs.

Vlad reaches up and takes my neck in one hand. He grips it firmly, the other hand slipping over my stomach and between my legs.

"Open up," he says. "I'm gonna make you come."

I part my thighs as wide as possible, dropping my head back and groaning as his fingertips brush my clit.

"That's it. Atta girl." He bumps his cock against my aching entrance as he plays with me, sending jolts of ecstasy through me. "You know what my wife is gonna get? Fucked by her husband, that's what. Damn hard. But you gotta give me those cute moans first."

His fingers work my clit, pressing harder and picking up a rhythm. My climax gathers, heat moving through my core, and I find my voice.

"I'm gonna come." I try to look at Vlad, but his grip on my throat is relentless. "Keep doing that."

He releases his hold on my neck and thrusts his hand into my hair, turning my head so he can kiss me. I cry out into his mouth as I come, fluid gushing from my pussy as he whips my clit with his fingers. He thrusts his tongue into my mouth and, with a smooth roll of his hips, buries his cock inside my still-spasming pussy. I gasp with shock, and he laughs.

"Yeah, give me all of it," he says. "You can come again for me, can't you? Give me what I want, like a good girl."

He places both hands on my waist to hold me in place, sliding me along his thick length. I'm still reeling from my orgasm, but my pussy isn't done yet, and a second explosion is on its way. Vlad is working up, too, his thrusts becoming firmer and faster.

"Fucking perfection," he says. "Touch your clit for me, Morgana. Tell me when you're ready to go again, and ride me through it."

It's too much. The feeling is running away with me. I rub my tender clit, and as Vlad bottoms out inside me again, I realize it's happening. Pleasure smashes through my body, making my legs shake.

"I'm coming!"

Vlad needs no further encouragement. He holds onto me tightly and hammers me like a man possessed. I squat over him, my quad muscles burning as I bounce.

"Take it." His cock thickens inside me. "Such a good girl." He groans as he comes, pinning my hips to his so he can make me take every drop.

I disentangle myself and lie beside him, my body aching all over.

"That was amazing," I say. "Aren't you worried I'm one of your baby-trap women? You never asked if I'm on birth control."

Vlad looks at me. "There are two answers to that question. First, I don't think you'd do something like that. You aren't the type. And you don't even *like* me."

I smile. "And the other answer?"

He strokes my arm. "The thought of filling you with my come and getting you pregnant tipped me over the edge." He grins at my shocked expression. "I'd love to fuck a baby into you, Morgana. *Are* you on birth control?"

"Yes," I say. "The pill."

"Shame." He raises an eyebrow. "If you decide to stay with me, you won't take that anymore."

"One thing at a time, Vladi."

By the time I return from the bathroom, Vlad is asleep. I lie beside him, listening to his breathing.

I could stay with him. Have his children, be his wife for real. Time will tell whether my husband's feelings for me are genuine, but there's hope in my heart.

He still frightens me a little, though. I allow myself an ironic smile.

I could be a good bratva wife, after all.

33

Three hours earlier...

Cassius

So he used the same clean-up crew for two murder scenes? Trusov asks. "How careless."

"Perhaps he was trying to keep Serra's murder quiet." I light a cigar. "It wasn't him who organized the disposal of Hektor and his men. That would explain a mistake like that. It's a minor error, but it was all I needed. I found one of the guys and he told me what I needed to know."

"So it appears Vladimir Kislev killed Hektor *and* Serra. Do we know why?"

"No idea." I blow a smoke ring. "Hektor was probably being mouthy with the wrong people. He was an idiot, Ira. Why you trusted him, I'll never know."

"His father was a good friend of mine," Trusov says, glaring at me. "So watch your fucking mouth."

Asshole. He never misses a chance to remind me I'm just a hired hand.

When I first got out of prison, he talked a good game. Waxed lyrical about me being family, his right-hand man, and all that bullshit. But I have no hold over him. I'm an employee. His son will inherit his bratva, and that fucker hates me.

My father's words intrude on my thoughts.

You're a little bitch, Cass. Easy to push around. Look what happens when I shove you like this—

"Are you listening to me?" Trusov asks.

"Sorry, Boss." I raise my palm in deference. "What do you want me to do?"

"I can't ask you to kill the new pakhan of New York's most powerful bratva," he says. "The game has changed. But he still murdered one of my men without discussing the matter with me first, and that's poor form. I'll admit Hektor was prone to stupidity, but whatever offense he caused could have been resolved amicably." Trusov picks up his whiskey, swilling it around the glass. "Meet with Vladimir and tell him I want to understand what happened here. I can't let the matter go, but he's not some street scum, and I'd be interested in hearing his side of the story."

"What if he decides to kill me, too?" I ask, stubbing the cigar out on the arm of the chair. "You could just call him."

"I don't fucking *know* him," he says, irritation creeping into his voice. "I will not ring him and arrange a meeting. You're not a pakhan and never will be, but believe me—that's not how it's done."

I keep my expression neutral, but I'm seething inside. Trusov was rattled to discover that the man I've been hunting is also a bratva leader, but he's behaving like an absolute pussy. I know damn well what he's worried about —he thinks Hektor pissed this Kislev guy off royally, and it's gonna be us on the back foot. He's happy to risk me getting murdered just so he can gauge the fucking mood?

Okay, fine. But I may have an ace in the hole.

I know of someone with influence over this situation. Whether that will benefit Trusov or just me remains to be seen.

"Did your informant have any useful info about the family?" Trusov asks.

"Only basic stuff. Vlad Kislev got married today, and his father Sergey died within hours of the ceremony."

"His wife knew Hektor, maybe?"

I laugh. "Unless Kislev married a whore, I doubt it. Apparently, he arranged it pretty hastily, but I didn't look into that. It didn't seem relevant."

Trusov knocks back his whiskey and grimaces. "This is where your inexperience tells, Cassius. If I'd known who we were dealing with, I'd never have given you this job, but you may as well see it through now." He leans forward, pointing at me. "But don't ignore the details. They can be the difference between life and death."

34

Two weeks later...

Morgana

The house is full of flowers.

Rivals and associates of the Kislevs sent bouquets of all shapes and sizes. Was the goal to send the most enormous and ostentatious arrangement possible to curry favor with Vlad? If so, he's not fooled.

The last two weeks have been a strange mix of blissful and tense. Yet, in some ways, things have never been better for me.

My parents are at the villa in Tuscany, soaking up the sunshine. My mom's health is much improved, and she's enjoying the outdoors, reading her romance novels under the shade of the lemon trees. I wish I were there, too, but

Vlad doesn't want me anywhere he isn't. There's an ominous feeling of impending trouble weighing everyone down.

Josie is working as an admin at Kislev Enterprises. She refused to be chased out of the city by an unknown threat, even when I reminded her that Italy is full of Italians. Specifically, hot Italian men. I couldn't persuade her, though, and I suspect it's because she wants to stay close to Sasha. He's been helping her learn the ropes in her new job, which everyone finds hilarious because Sasha knows precisely bupkis about investments and acquisitions. Vlad is just grateful to have his brother out of his hair.

Arman and David have divided their efforts between the dual goals of locating Cassius and resolving the issue with Hektor's boss, whoever he is. No one sees much of Avel, but when he shows his face, he asks Vlad what he can do to help. I guess the kid just wants to feel useful.

The one who's doing best is Lilyana. She'll return from her walk soon, and I love hearing how it went.

I'm ready to go, but we aren't due to leave for another hour. I took ages getting ready, so I could keep out of the way, but I couldn't hide in the suite any longer.

I vaguely recognize some of the people here from our wedding reception. Vlad told me they were members of the *komissiya*, sometimes called 'the top table' in English. They are the most respected elders of bratva society, tasked with imposing a code of honor and order on their chaotic, criminal kingdom. I don't envy them.

I use my new camera to take pictures of the flowers. There's something doleful about the juxtaposition of their fragile beauty and the somber figures standing amongst them. One of the *komissiya* men sees me and frowns.

"Don't take my photo, girl," he says, reaching for the camera. A hand lands on my shoulder from behind, and I realize it's Vlad.

"Put your hands on my wife, Igor, and I'll bury two men today. I may not even do you the courtesy of killing you beforehand."

Igor scowls. "Your father was a great man, Vladimir. He would never have threatened a superior, especially not in defense of a woman."

"*This* woman is *my* wife, and she takes orders from no one except me." Vlad's voice is low and even. "Morgana Georgevna Kisleva is her name. Use it. Or don't fucking speak to her at all. She has no business with you. If you have a problem, come to me."

"You're having a tough time, Vlad. So I'll let it go. But you need to remember what's expected of you."

Igor backs out of the lounge. Vlad wraps me in his arms and kisses my forehead.

"Sorry about that, *lisichka*. You look beautiful in black." He nods at the flowers crammed into vases and piled on the table. "Were you taking pictures of these? There's a story behind them."

Vlad encourages me to take my camera everywhere we go, and for every moment I capture, he insists I write something, too. He bought me a stunning Montblanc notebook, and now I scribble down my thoughts and a photo description.

Vlad picks up a bunch of lilies. "Look here, Morgana." he counts them quickly, "thirty flowers are in the bouquet. Every arrangement here has an even number of stems. Do you know why?" I shake my head, and he smiles. "It's a Slavic tradition from way back. Even numbers represent the end of the life cycle. Russians love flowers, but unless they are for a funeral, you must give an odd number in a bouquet." His face darkens. "After my parents were married, Papa took my mother's wedding bouquet and extracted a single rose, crushing it beneath his heel. He said it was only fitting since her life was effectively over."

Vlad and I have talked a great deal about his mother. Sergey's death is the psychological equivalent of opening the windows and letting fresh air blow through. In those optimistic moments, I see the person Vlad is inside—the passionate, sensitive, deep man his Mama knew he could be. At other times, he's distant, hard to engage, brooding. I know he's going through something, and I'm putting it down to the lack of closure. He'll put his father in the ground today, and then, maybe, he'll stop trying to bury himself.

"I don't have my notebook with me," I say, placing my palm on his cheek, "but something tells me I'll remember that." My heart aches at the sorrow in his eyes. "Just get through today. It'll be alright."

"The issue with Hektor's boss will come to a head soon," he says suddenly, letting go of me and dropping the flowers on the armchair. "His man will find me, or I'll find him, but that shit will be dealt with. I'm not worried about that. But I have to find your prick of an ex." He throws me a look. "I can't relax until I know he's dead."

"Not now." I take his hand. "It's not the time."

Lilyana bustles through the front door, Arman behind her. "Vladi!" she says, weaving through the floral forest toward us. "We walked six blocks, and I got my own coffee."

"Yeah, but you didn't get me one, did you?" Arman says. "I was there, protecting you, and what thanks do I get?"

Lili giggles. "Sorry." She holds her cup out to him. "You want the rest of this?"

"*Tsvetok*, that's not coffee. It's basically a milkshake."

Lili shrugs. "Whatever." A tiny line appears between her eyebrows when she sees her big brother's expression. "Come on, Vladi." She slips her arm into his. "Everyone is leaving for the church. We can't be the last to arrive. And for once, I'm not afraid. Papa's gone, and I have you."

Vlad smiles at her. "Always." He reaches for me, taking my hand. "Let's get this over with."

35

Vlad

It's hard to keep the correct expression on my face. David walks around the restaurant, shaking hands and accepting condolences while I sit alone, nursing a drink and looking like the dutiful bereaved son.

I told Morgana I was not prepared to let her go far from my side because I believed she may be in danger. That's not the only reason, though. While she needs me, she won't leave, and I don't have to face the harsh reality that snaps at my heels.

Morgana doesn't *have* to stay with me. She already has ten million dollars in her private account and has kept her side of the bargain. Papa's will was read last week, and I made the financial and business transfers shortly after. It's all in my name, and I can do anything. I no longer need to be married.

That's a fucking lie. But I don't need just *any* wife. I need *my* wife. The woman who went way past her brief and soothed my soul when my demons came out to play.

I didn't know Papa's death would change me. Now that he's gone, I thought I'd be free and unburdened, but I'm troubled. My feelings for Morgana are deepening, and I'm drifting further from the ideal image of a pakhan that my father instilled in me.

"Women are leeches," he would say. "They want your money, but it's more than that—they'd reach into your bones and scoop out the marrow if they could. They are parasites, and it's your job to get what you need from them without letting them latch onto you."

He was full of shit. But it's hard to turn away from a future I recognize and embrace the unknown.

Mama wasn't a parasite. Neither is Morgana. It's Papa who bled everyone around him dry.

As he was lowered into the earth, I felt nothing but contempt. I threw a handful of soil into the grave and muttered a half-assed prayer, but I wouldn't have the audacity to ask God for favors, least of all on my father's behalf.

Most mourners were at the wedding, creating a bizarre déjà vu. Unlike the reception, many couples have their children with them. I haven't seen kids playing since the twins were tiny, and the sight pulls at my heart. I glimpse Morgana across the room, talking to Josie, and my anxiety eases. As long as I know where she is, I'm fine. I'm not worried about anything happening at Papa's wake—it's unforgivably rude to cause a ruckus at a funeral.

I'm contemplating getting a top-up when a man sits down opposite me.

"Good afternoon, Mr. Kislev."

"Do I know you, *tovarishch*?"

I take the man's extended hand. He's younger than me, with a wiry strength that's easy to underestimate. His smile is brief and tight.

"We haven't met," he says, "but we have a shared problem."

I don't fucking like this guy. He's too unctuous, too self-assured. He walked into my father's funeral dinner to talk business with me?

"So get on with it." I finish my drink. "I don't have all day."

"I am the one you've been looking for." He leans forward, raising his eyebrows. "You know. The one who's been asking questions about the pimp you killed."

"You're Hektor's boss? Wait, no. You're running errands for someone else. Your boss wouldn't come here."

The man tries to smile again, but I see his irritation. He doesn't enjoy being a nobody. I know an overreaching underling when I see one.

"I represent a powerful individual." The man sits back in his chair. "He's a pakhan in Chicago. Hektor would have told you that. What did he do to make you kill him rather than discuss it?"

"You mean apart from peddling vice on my territory? I don't have to explain myself to anyone. Tell your boss to come and talk to me."

"He's unhappy." A smirk curls his lip, and I resist punching him. "He feels you owe him an explanation and compensation, too. He didn't allow Hektor to infiltrate your turf, but he would have reprimanded him and spared us all this."

"I'm not interested." I push my chair away from the table. "Run home and tell your employer he needs to keep you on a short leash and out of my fucking business. I'll let it go. But I don't want to see you in my city again."

I glance at Morgana. She's waving at me, but her arm drops to her side as I watch. She snatches at the table's edge, trying to stay on her feet as Josie supports her. A keening scream of anguish fills the air, silencing everyone except the children playing on the floor nearby, who continue happily with their game.

The stranger sees Morgana and breaks into laughter. I get to my feet, preparing to strangle him.

"I wouldn't," he says. "I have a pistol pointing at you beneath the table."

I could grab my own gun from its holster in a nanosecond, but he'd be faster. I tear my eyes from my screaming wife and sit down again.

"Kill me, and you'll never leave here alive."

"I know. How many kids could I shoot first?" He grins with what looks like genuine glee. "I reckon I could take out a couple before anyone got to me. Maybe Morgana too?"

Morgana is sobbing her heart out. I hear Josie pleading with her, trying to find out what's wrong.

But I have worked it out.

The man stands, revealing the gun in his hand. He backs toward the restaurant door, his gun trained on the oblivious children.

He cocks his head at me and tuts. "The innocent virgin bratva pussy you could have, and you get hitched to this well-used bitch? It's not a good look for a pakhan to marry a call girl."

Sasha catches my eye, but I shake my head. Then the man is gone, tearing down the street. Sasha bolts, but I lunge and grab him.

"Let him go. We can't risk a shoot-out in broad daylight, not with the fucking families here. And our relationship with the cops relies on keeping our business off the streets."

Mothers dash to the children, cradling them in their arms.

"Do you think that's why he chose this moment to accost you?" Sasha asks.

"I don't think he knew what he was getting himself into." I put my hand on his shoulder. "Stay here with David. I can't believe the fucker said that in front of everyone, and I'm in no frame of mind to hear any more about it. I'm taking my wife away from here."

I go to Morgana's side. She's sitting on the floor, shaking and hiccuping, her breathing shallow. I pull her head onto my chest and hold her.

"Vladi." Her words are nothing more than a hoarse whisper. "That was Cassius. Why was he talking to you? Don't let him take me!"

"Shh. You're going nowhere, *lisichka*."

She laughs through her tears. "Isn't that the truth? I'm with *you*, waiting for a happy ending that may never come. And now *he's* here, and he'll kill me this time—"

"You think I'd let that happen?"

Josie puts her hand on my arm. "Easy, Vladi. She's just scared."

I scoop my hands under Morgana's legs and get to my feet, lifting her against my chest as she wraps her arms around my neck. I'm reminded of that first night when she screamed in her sleep, and I consoled her.

She turns to look at me, and I press my forehead to hers.

"Take me away from here," she whispers.

36

Vlad

Morgana drinks the tea Dulcie made but says little. I can't bear to look at her, so I distract myself by raising hell.

"David, I want this shit dealt with immediately," I say into my phone. "Find out who that asshole works for. I want a name tonight."

"You shouldn't have let him go," David says.

"I was caught off guard. Don't you think our bratva would have had even bigger problems if we'd killed innocent people trying to get to one errand boy? He's blown his cover, so it's only a matter of time. Find him and bring his stupid ass to me."

"What about his boss?"

"Arman is questioning anyone who has connections to the jail or Chicago. Won't take long for someone to give us the information."

David sighs. "Stop and think, Vladi. Cassius Jackson is Morgana's ex. I get it—you wanna make him suffer. But your lack of foresight brought him back into her life. If you hadn't killed Hektor, none of this would have happened."

I see red. "You think I don't fucking know that? Fuck yourself, David. I will protect my wife and my bratva however I see fit."

"You mentioned your wife first, Vladi. Remember when you told me you wouldn't put a woman before your duty?"

I hang up.

David can't seize power from me. It'd take balls he hasn't got.

He'd have to kill me, and my dear old *dyadya* hasn't the stomach for it. All hell would break loose. But sometimes I wish he'd try because then I could justify beating the shit out of him. Until now, he's done nothing more than bait me, but I'm losing patience fast.

Morgana is curled up on the lounge chair, a shearling throw around her shoulders. I've never seen her so meek, and it breaks my heart. My beautiful wife's spark was extinguished by the merest glimpse of the bastard who traumatized her.

She told me all about Cassius. How she took photos of her injuries and kept call recordings and text messages. When he went too far, she found the strength to go to the cops. Cassius had priors for domestic violence and was on his last chance, so the judge threw the book at him, giving him a five-year sentence.

I touch Morgana's shoulder, and she shrinks away.

"You know what I saw in my nightmares, Vladi?

"What, *lisichka*?"

"I saw *him*. Laughing at me. Beating me. Telling me I didn't deserve better." She wipes her eye with the back of her hand. "And I dreamed he would come back. That I'd turn around one day, and he'd be right there." She gives a hollow laugh. "And there I was, thinking my dreams would never come true."

"I'm certain he didn't know you were my wife," I say. "His reaction when he saw you was genuine. He came to talk to me about Hektor, not to find you." Rage takes hold, and I kick the table, cracking it. "I'll kill the bastard, I swear."

"How will you find him?"

"I would have found him, anyway. I was looking for Cassius Jackson when I thought he was only your scumbag ex. Arman always said Hektor's boss might find me first and send someone to fuck me up. Interesting that he sent no army."

"You think his boss will fight for him?" Morgana's eyes are wide with fear.

"No. Inter-city mob wars are a special kind of hell. If it were me, I'd hand the cunt over myself as a goodwill gesture. I guess we'll find out."

I pace the floor, my head in pieces.

Morgana may never have seen that scumbag again if not for me. I pulled her into my violent world when I could have left her alone. She's done something to *me*, too. She breezed into my dysfunctional life and *changed* me. All that shit that mattered before is worth nothing if my wife suffers.

What the hell have we done to one other?

"You don't have to do this for me," Morgana says.

"Cassius disrespected me. Don't you understand what could happen to my bratva—to my *family*—if I don't stand firm?"

I'm yelling like it's all her fault. And maybe it is. She encouraged me to lighten up, to let her in.

"Don't take it out on me," she says. "I'm your family now, so I'm in danger, too. But I'm at your side when I could just leave you."

The thought is like a punch to the gut. "Not if I didn't permit it."

"Vladi, you could force me to stay with you, but I can still freeze you out. I could turn you out of our bed, and you'd go back to that couch because you—"

"Don't say it." I squeeze my eyes closed, trying to block her out. "Don't. You're my wife, my downfall, my obsession. People can see my weakness." I press my thumbs into my temples. "You gave me hope I could be better than my father. Why did you *do* that, Morgana? All you had to do was play your part, but you made me love you."

Oh, sweet Jesus. I didn't know I felt it until now, but it's the truest thing I've ever said.

"You love me?"

She comes to me, and I pull her into my arms. "Yes," I murmur. "I told you, *lisichka*—I didn't have far to go. You enthralled me from the start. I stole you and forced you into a situation you didn't want, and you handled it with grace and fortitude. You saw past my bullshit to the man inside and coaxed out the best in me. And no one *made* you do that. It's your nature."

"Why not let *your* nature shine through, Vladi?" Morgana winds her hands through my hair. "You're desperate for Sergey's shitty teachings to mean something because, deep down, you're still that kid who wants to make his father proud."

"I'm not afraid of going to war." I kiss her tenderly. "But loving you scares the shit out of me. I lost the purest love I ever had, and it hurt so much. I don't know what would happen to me if I lost *you* too. Sure, I'd burn the world to ashes in a maelstrom of vengeance, but it wouldn't ease the pain. I know that all too well."

37

Cassius

Fucking *fuck* it. *I'm dead.*

I cannot believe my slut ex is Vladimir Kislev's wife. I fully intended to call on her one day and make her pay for what she did to me, but she's fucked me over *again*, just by existing.

Her husband will no longer give a shit about making amends with Trusov. It's personal now. I hurt his wife, and he'll lay waste to everything in his path to get to me. Calling her a whore in front of all his friends wasn't the smartest thing I've ever done, and now that I'm calming down, I can see I've only worsened my problem. Anger issues aside, I'm not dumb. I know how this will end.

Trusov was happy to let Hektor do his networking, and when that didn't work out, I made a show of strength on his behalf. Whatever happened to leading from the front?

I was so keen to infiltrate a bratva that I didn't do my homework. The old man's cowardice will probably get me killed. Trusov will bend over and let Vladimir Kislev fuck him if it means avoiding a fight.

Unless I play my ace and win. It's the only chance I have to save my hide. Maybe I'll hit the jackpot.

David Kislev flings open the passenger door and gets in, glancing around as he does so.

"No one's looking, for fuck's sake." I pull away from the curb and join the late evening traffic. "I appreciate you taking my call."

"I don't know how the fuck you got my number," he says, "but I guess you have similar resources to us. What do you want to discuss?"

"Like I said—the future of your bratva. It's in trouble, right? Your new pakhan is killing people whenever he feels like it, not trying to keep the peace. He threatened me, and I'm just a messenger."

"You're here to save us all, is that it?" David puts a gun on his knee. "I'm not stupid. Say what you came to say, and I'll decide whether to kill you."

It was a hell of a risk to contact David and meet him, but the fact he came alone says he's intrigued by what I said on the phone. He's caught a whiff of an opportunity. I only have to sell it.

"It's like I told you. I used to fuck Vladimir's wife, and I knocked her about too. He clearly knew about it but didn't know I was looking for him. And seriously—do you really think I'd have waltzed in and made demands if I'd known I would see my ex wearing his fucking wedding ring?"

"He loves her." David sounds weary. "He's made nothing but stupid decisions because of that woman. My brother Sergey did all he could to teach Vlad how to be strong, but he failed."

It's time to roll the dice.

"If Vladimir were... removed, you would take charge. Correct?"

David pauses before answering. "Yes. I'm not prepared to kill him, if that's what you're asking."

"Of course not. I dispose of Vlad and his wife, and you take control of the bratva. In return, you let me go back to *my* bratva and live my life. Fifty million dollars will encourage me to keep my mouth shut."

David sighs. "That's the deal, is it?

A second roll is needed. I have to take the gamble.

"My boss will capitulate as soon as Vladimir challenges him. He won't go to war over me—I don't have enough value. You need your nephew and his wife dead to get what you're due, with no suspicion leveled at you. Who could you trust?"

"I can't trust *you*," he says, glaring at me. "I don't fucking know you."

"That's the whole point, David. Vlad wants to kill me, and he'll never stop hunting. You said so yourself. Who will cross him for me? You and I have a common goal."

"So if Vladi dies, you are off the hook."

Exactly, you old cunt. Now stop hemming and hawing and get with the fucking program. I want that bitch and her pretty-boy husband begging for their lives.

I stay silent, letting the idea percolate. If David Kislev has any integrity, he'll put that pistol to my head and blow my brains out.

"What exactly would I have to do?" he asks.

"Nothing much. Just tell a few lies."

38

Morgana

We lie face to face in our bed, naked. We've done this many times over the last two weeks before or after having sex, but the closeness is enough for now.

Seeing Cassius has dragged me back into the hell he put me through. The manipulation, the lies, the violence.

I remember all too well the new relationship energy when I thought Cassius was amazing and we'd be together forever. The L word tripped off my tongue so quickly back then. Months later, when I was looking for good camouflage makeup to hide my bruises, I would think of those early days and curse my naïve heart for seeing only what it wanted to see.

I want to tell Vlad I love him too, but fear holds my tongue. He tried so hard to convince me he doesn't do love, and I was determined to prove him wrong. If he were right all along, I would have no one to blame but myself.

Is history repeating itself? Am I destined to love men who only view me as a possession, something to own but never to cherish?

Vlad runs his hand down my arm. "Seeing him today really messed you up, didn't it?"

"I feel better now." I smile as he strokes my back. "And you seem strangely calm."

"I was angry about what that fucker did to you." Vlad props himself up on his elbow. I got caught up in myself, brooding over the pain my father inflicted on me and livid he didn't get his comeuppance. But I was wrong."

I frown. "I don't understand."

"Papa is dead, and for the first time, I'm *alive*. Falling in love is the best 'fuck you' ever."

He means it when he says he loves me. I see it in his eyes. Even if it doesn't last, right now, it's real.

"I love you too, Vladi."

He pushes me away so he can look into my eyes. "Fuck me, really? I never thought you would. I'm an asshole, Morgana. How many ways have I shown you that?" He furrows his brow. "You have fuckawful taste in men, you know."

My Vladi. Yes, he's toxic. He's arrogant, brooding, and occasionally downright difficult, and that's before I get to the murderous possessiveness. But under all that bullshit beats a tender heart, yearning for someone to accept his shattered soul and not judge him.

I roll into his arms, my head on his chest. He tweaks my nipple gently, and I bite my lip. "How could I not love you?" I ask. "You're *not* a complete asshole, as much as you tried to convince me otherwise. You just thought you *had* to be one, and that's a different matter." I grin. "I must confess—I kinda miss hating you."

"Yeah. That was an interesting five minutes."

"Fuck you!" I slap his chest playfully. "So I had the hots for you, fine. But who did the kidnapping? You barely said a word to me before you carried my ass away like a sack of flour. That is not what is meant by a pickup line."

"Why don't you pretend to hate me, just for fun?" Vlad brushes my nipple with his fingertip. "Tell me what you imagined me doing to you when you touched yourself."

My body quickens at his touch. "I imagined you being rough. I guessed right, didn't I?"

"I'm versatile." Vlad slips his hand between my thighs. "I can ruin you any time; if that's what I want, there'll be no stopping me. But if you wanna give me orders and make me your slave, I'm into it." He slips a finger between my folds, and I draw a sharp breath. "I'm the king now, Morgana, and you are my queen. But a single word from your lips will bring me to my knees. Nobody else has that kind of power over me and never will."

Vlad's fingertip dips into my entrance, finding my wet core. He draws out the moisture and spreads it onto my clit, massaging it with the length of his finger. "Here." He lifts my leg, resting it on his hip. "Get closer, and let me do my thing." He cups my ass and pulls me to him, his erection hot against my stomach. "That's better. Now look at me."

It's intense. Vlad's tongue invades my mouth, his kisses slow and deep. I slide my arm around him, feeling his solid back muscles flexing under my palm. My other hand grasps his cock, sliding him over my wet pussy, and he groans.

"We can fuck in this position," he murmurs. "I'm big enough." He stops playing with my clit and scoots lower to tongue my nipple, lifting my leg higher until my knee is beside his ear. His hot tip nudges my entrance, and he holds me still, rocking himself into me inch by inch.

He feels so good, stretching and filling my hungry pussy, but I don't want to give him what he wants. Not yet. I squeeze my internal muscles, pushing him out of me.

"Jesus fuck, *lisichka*. Let me in!"

"No. I hate you. Remember?"

A shit-eating grin splits his face. "I know, baby. Why don't you sit on my face and tell me all about it?"

He read my damn mind. How does he *do* that?

Vlad swats my ass as I scramble out of his grasp. He guides me into position, my thighs on either side of his head.

"Sit down, hold on, and let me please you," he says.

I rest my hands on the bed rail, and he holds my hip bone to steady me. I moan as he wraps his lips around my sensitive clit, sucking it firmly. His free hand reaches behind me, teasing my entrance from behind.

"You're so wet," he says, his mouth moving against my pussy lips. He laps my clit with the flat of his tongue, and I arch my back as pleasure sears my nerves. "And you taste so delicious. I could eat you for hours."

He draws a slick fingertip along the valley between my ass cheeks and finds my smallest hole. He rubs it, stimulating the tender flesh, and I gasp.

"Oh, my wife likes her ass played with?" Vlad rewards me with a rapid lash of his tongue, and I clench my thighs around his head.

If I could speak, I'd tell him I've never had anything in my ass. I didn't know it could feel good until five seconds ago when he touched me there.

Vlad dips into my entrance with two fingers, gathering a good amount of juice and slathering it over my ass. He slips his first two fingers deep into my pussy, and I groan with satisfaction as his knuckles catch on my sensitive spots. He gets a rhythm going before broaching my asshole with his thumb, working my clit to help me relax.

"Easy," he says. "Let's get both your pretty little holes in play, shall we?"

His well-lubricated thumb eases past the first ring of muscle. My mouth hangs open as he slides it home.

"Good girl. Is my wife a greedy little slut for me?"

I get no opportunity to respond before he releases my hip and stuffs his fingers into my mouth. He thrusts them into my throat with the same rhythm as his other hand, still reaming my pussy and ass simultaneously.

"Air-tight." He grips my jaw and pulls my face down to see my eyes. "You look so gorgeous with all your holes filled."

My body is alight with sensation, sending surges of bliss up my spine, and Vlad's fingers in my mouth feel so dirty and wrong. Vlad works my clit with short, rapid sucks, and my pussy begins to spasm. I pump my hips, pushing my holes onto Vlad's surging fingers. He never lets up on my clit, and as my climax peaks, he yanks his fingers from my throat and wraps them around my neck, gripping hard.

"Ride my mouth," he says. "Your pleasure is mine. Give it to me."

39

Vlad

Morgana is still whimpering as I flip her onto her back. My cock is agony, the veins straining under the pressure, and I jerk it for a moment to take the edge off.

The man who hurt my wife sat a couple of feet away, and I fucking let him go. I said it was because there were too many innocent bystanders, but part of me wanted to handle him on my own terms. Shooting the bastard is too fucking easy.

I can't erase the knowledge that Cassius Jackson put his hands on my Morgana. As much as I don't want to hurt her, I need to mark her in my own way.

I loom over her, pushing her legs high and wide. Her pink pussy opens like a flower, her juicy come making it glisten. I position my raging cock at her entrance and slam into her in one deep thrust, grabbing her thighs so she doesn't slide off the bed. She cries out in shock.

"Oh, my God!"

"He won't help you, *lisichka*." I sit back on my heels, pulling her to bounce on my cock. "He washed his hands of me and my behavior long ago. You wanna appeal to a deity for mercy, see if The Devil will take your calls."

I grip her neck, and her pulse flutters under my palm. She's a mess, her face streaked with spit and tears where she choked on my fingers. I'm fucking her too hard, but I couldn't ease up even if I wanted to. It's the release we both need.

As I wonder whether it's too much, Morgana's fingers reach for her clit.

"Open your eyes." I slide my hand to the back of her neck and pull her upright, winding my fingers around her hair. "Look me in the eye while I rail you."

Her amber eyes burn as she stares at me. The knot in my stomach loosens as my climax gathers, suffusing my body with a wave of warmth, and I pound her with everything I've got.

Morgana's eyes roll as a scream of ecstasy escapes her. "Don't stop," she says, her fingers a blur on her clit. "I'm coming again!"

Her clinging heat envelops me, drawing me in, and it's too much. With a growl, I pull my cock free and grab it, tugging her head back as I do so.

"You are mine," I say, pumping my cock. "Not his. *Never* his."

All my rage and stress drain away as I come, decorating Morgana's face with my seed. She licks her lips, tasting me.

"Don't lose that," I say. I take her chin in my hand. "Open your mouth."

She does as she's told, and I lick the come from her face, sweeping it into her mouth with my tongue.

"Now swallow."

She gulps and smiles. "That's somehow disgusting and incredibly hot."

I shrug. "That's me to a T."

~

I leave Morgana dozing and head downstairs. To my surprise, Sasha's car is outside. He's in the gym, counting plates onto the leg press machine.

"I didn't expect to find you working on your wheels," I say.

"Morgana's ex was quite the buzzkill." Sasha gets into position and tests the weight. "The wake was even deader than Papa, so I ended it early. No one minded under the circumstances." He grins. "We are gonna get a rep for throwing shitty parties. At least you didn't kill anyone this time."

"I fucking *should* have." I hand him a drink. "Did you bring the twins home?"

He nods. "Lilyana was pretty upset and went straight to bed. Avel wanted to go with Arman, but *dyadya* David said no way." He extends his legs and winces. "David did us proud today. He made up for our piss poor acting skills and played the part of a bereaved brother when he didn't give a shit either."

I suspected David and his motives for getting on my case, but I'm now confident he has nothing up his sleeve. Papa has been dead for two weeks, and my uncle hasn't pulled any dodgy stunts or undermined me since. Pragmatically, he has no means to launch a coup against me anyway—anyone he approached would rat him out to me immediately, hoping for a handsome reward.

He thinks he has to lean on me because I no longer have my father. Perhaps I should bring him on board permanently and give him some of the power he craves. All the old man wants is his own little kingdom; who can blame him?

I'm glad I shared none of my suspicions with my family. We don't have to play Papa's mind games, not anymore.

"Yeah, credit where it's due," I say. "David's a grumpy bastard, but he has our best interests at heart."

My phone rings, and I answer it without looking. "Talk to me."

"Prepare to be fucking happy, Vladi," Arman says. "Nico the Flea behaved exactly like a parasite should and put his survival first. I went to ask some general questions, but the little cunt was so jumpy it got me wondering. I barely tickled him before he gave up the info—I reckon Lili could have got him to sing."

"So, what's the news?"

"Nico and Cassius know each other from way back. It's him who directed Cassius to Serra." Irritation creeps into his voice. "You called in a clean-up after killing that fat Italian prick, and Cassius watched them. Nico knows all those guys, and it didn't take Cassius long to find a man who cleaned up

Hektor too. That's how he figured out it was you. Every single one of those poor bastards is dead. Did you know that?"

No, I fucking didn't.

"Tell me you got a name."

"I did better than that. I got you a name and a number. The boys in blue came through for us tonight, so send the Commissioner a hamper or something."

"Good work, *tovarishch*." Sasha gives me a questioning look, and I reply with a thumbs-up. "Where's David?"

"Fuck knows. I left him a message. He'll show up."

"Yeah, he can take care of himself. Now get off the line and send me the deets. I need to fucking shout at someone."

I leave Sasha to finish his workout and head back to the suite. Morgana is in the shower, and I shed my clothes, jumping in with her.

"Vladi!" she says, laughing. "Shut the door. It's freezing!"

"I'll warm you up." I pull her to me, enjoying her smooth skin on mine. "You've lived your self-love fantasy. Now it's my turn."

∽

When I call Ira Trusov's office the following morning, someone puts me straight through to him. He must have been expecting to hear from me.

He wasn't expecting what I just told him.

"I knew nothing of this, Vladimir." I wonder how old he is. The strain in his voice suggests he's ancient or smokes like a chimney. "If I had, I would never—"

"Let me make this absolutely clear," I say. "Cassius Jackson may have been useful. Maybe he was loyal, reliable, whatever. But none of that matters. He hurt my wife, so now he's a corpse-in-waiting and a tremendous liability for *you*. Do you understand?"

"I will call him off. Bring him back to Chicago and not further trouble you or your wife."

"So you *don't* fucking understand."

David, Sasha, and Arman all stare at me as I speak. It might be rude of me to call a business meeting over breakfast, but I need them to hear this.

"I'm troubled by Cassius's existence, Ira," I say. "I don't like that he breathes the same air as me. You say you didn't know his connection to my wife, and I believe you, but I still want him dead. At my hands, ideally. Deliver him to me."

"I didn't want to fight over Hektor, not with you. Cassius is not taking my calls. He isn't that stupid. He knows damn well I will not go to war for him."

"Hektor threatened my wife and tried to coerce her into prostitution." I let the enormity of the offense sink in.

"*Bozhe moy*." Ira heaves a sigh. "I understand why you killed him. I am at your disposal. If Cassius shows his face here in Chicago, I will have him brought to you. Is that acceptable?"

"Yes. You're a wise man, Ira. Let's talk again in better circumstances."

Ira's relief is palpable, even over the phone. "*Da*, Vladimir Sergeyovich Kislev. Good morning."

"*Dobroye utro.*" I hang up and address my family. "Trusov guarantees Cassius will not be given quarter on his home turf, so get the word out. Anyone who shelters Cassius Jackson risks death at my hands. I'll pay ten million dollars for his corpse, twenty million for him alive. I'll address no bratva business until this cunt is in our custody."

Sasha almost chokes on his coffee. "*Brat*, that's insane. You're the new pakhan, and our associates expect you to show them favor. Cement old friendships, strengthen boundaries, reassure our allies that you have your eye on the ball."

I fix him with a glare. "So you'd better deal with this quickly, yes?"

"Don't give Vladi that shit, Sasha," David says. "It's not your place. It matters to him, so it matters to all of us."

My uncle is finally in my corner. *About time.*

Avel nods. "Fucking right."

I raise an eyebrow at him. "You keep out of it, *malchik*. I need no boy soldiers on the front lines." I stand, tossing my serviette on the table. "Everyone else—you know what to do."

We leave the kitchen, my brothers and David heading out to start the day's hunting. I go upstairs, intending to wake Morgana and give her an update, but she's nowhere to be found.

She went out without me? She knows what could happen. For all I know, Cassius has her right now.

A cold feeling of dread creeps up my spine. *Where the fuck is my wife?*

40

Morgana

The last time I went to the pond was the day Vlad and I met. My life was hanging by a thread, and he swept in and saved me. I just didn't realize it, and neither did he.

Arman usually insists on supervising Lili, but he's too anxious, too keen to bring her home to safety. When Vlad said he needed to hold a meeting this morning, I jumped at the chance to accompany his little sister on her walk. She's coming out of her shell, getting stronger and bolder daily.

Lili sits near the water's edge, weaving strands of grass. I join her.

"You don't need anyone to supervise you out here," I say. "When all this stuff with Cassius is over, I'll talk to Vladi and get him to let you out on your own. You're an adult, anyway. It's not up to him what you do."

She smiles. "He's afraid something will happen to me. I guess he thinks he has to keep me safe now because he didn't before. Not that I think it was his fault, but he never got over it."

"I know." I take her hand. "He'll get better."

"That's because of you. He's so happy, Morgana. Even with all this scary stuff happening, he's calm. Centered." She sighs. "Your love makes him strong. He'd never have believed that in a million years."

The sunshine bathes the treeline, dappling us with spots of bright light. I grab my camera and take a snap of Lili before she can stop me.

"Morgana!" She pulls a face. "Why?"

"It felt like a moment worth capturing." I make a frame with my fingers and look through at her, making her giggle. "You're free, Lili. Free from your father and his abusive hate. Vlad is changing, and the rest of the family is following because he's a leader. Did you ever think you'd sit peacefully by the pond and not feel anxious?"

"You're right. I am calm." Her eyes widen. "I can't remember feeling relaxed out in the world. There's so much I could do! I never thought about it before. Maybe I could be a concert pianist!"

My heart aches with pleasure to see her so happy. Her father made her believe she was defective and her family's shame. Although Vlad loved her, he was afraid and kept her close for her safety. It's as though she's emerging from her chrysalis, her painted wings drying and unfurling in the sun. Her future is shining on her, full of possibilities.

Josie appears on the path, waving. "I got your text and dashed out for a few minutes. Sasha is out of the office, and I have so much to do."

"How is the job?" I ask. "I don't really know what you do."

"I make dirty money nice and clean by sifting it through thousands of transactions and fake companies." She grins. "It's kinda satisfying. Every business and bank takes my call, no matter when I ring. The best thing about organized crime is you're never left on hold." She cocks her head at Lili. "When did you get released into the wild? Get a tan. Your perfect milky complexion is unacceptable."

Lili nods and gives Josie a military-style salute. "You and Sasha are a thing, right?" she asks.

Anguish flashes over Josie's features instantly before she shoves it down. "No. We're friends, and he's kinda my boss too, so it wouldn't be right."

"I knew Vladi was into Morgana before *he* did," Lili says, raising an eyebrow.

Josie laughs. "I'm not convinced you're a matchmaker extraordinaire based on one example." She glances at her watch. "Gotta go. I'm a successful Noo Yawk Siddy businesswoman and have no time for gadabouts like you two."

Josie dashes off, and we're about to make a move when I see Vlad storming toward us. His body language suggests he's unhappy; I have a good idea why.

"You scared the shit out of me! Your ex is out there somewhere, possibly looking for a chance to hurt you, and you're wandering around the fucking park?"

"We're sitting still, not wandering," Lili says. "It's okay, Vladi. Nothing happened. We got some iced tea and doughnuts and chilled out in the sunshine." She furrows her brow. "Until you showed up yelling, we were having a good time."

Vlad ignores her and addresses me. "You're a liability, Morgana. You can't protect Lili; even if you could, who is protecting *you*? Both of you are my responsibility to keep safe from harm, but you need to fucking listen to me."

Liliyana sniffs. She's trying not to cry. Doesn't he understand what this means to her?

"Stop it," I say. "Just shut up. Lili is fine, I'm fine. You can't always be there, Vlad. There's no level of control you could exert that would eliminate all risk."

"Alright." He exhales slowly. "But don't push me. I've put all our resources into finding Cassius, and until he's out of the picture, I'm extremely antsy." He turns to Lili. "I'm sorry. Was there something you wanted to do today?"

"No." Lili stands and stretches. "Let's go home."

∼

I wait until Lili goes to her room to ask the question.

"How did you know where we were?"

Vlad stops tinkering with the piano and stares at me. "What?"

"Don't give me that." I fold my arms. "You had no reason to assume we were in the park."

"Are you honestly surprised to learn I'm tracking you?" he asks. "I installed the software on your phone the day I brought you here. You're always leaving the damn thing lying around."

My mouth drops open. "And Lilyana?"

"She has a medic alert bracelet. It has a tracking chip in the strap."

"Vladi, normal people don't do that."

"I'm not a normal person." He stands and reaches for me. "This lifestyle is perilous, *lisichka*. And however much you wanna pretend you can do what you want, you can't. Not without taking precautions."

"Precautions like *this*?"

I open my blazer to reveal a compact pistol nestled at my hip. Vlad points at it.

"Holy fuck. Where did you get that?"

"I found the armory in the basement. You really ought to lock it. Did you think I wouldn't take matters into my own hands?"

He grins and reaches for the weapon, drawing it from the holster. He puts it in my hand. "Do you know how to fire it?"

I hold the gun out in front of me. "Like this. Don't worry, I won't point it at you."

"I'm not worried." He takes the pistol and taps the side. "*That* is the safety switch. You need the little red dot to be visible, or it won't fire."

I frown. "But when you killed Bruno, you just drew your gun and shot him without a pause."

"That's because *my* gun is a Glock and doesn't have safety." He raises an eyebrow. "I'm used to firearms, but you have no idea what you're doing, Morgana. I'm seriously pissed at you for carrying a gun without my knowledge. But you didn't shoot me, which is something."

"First time for everything." I raise an eyebrow, and he smirks. "Don't think you can keep me under lock and key just because you love me, Vladi. That's not how it works. I stay on my own terms."

He nods. "I understand. No gilded cage for you, and I'll teach you how to handle a pistol. But let me take out Cassius first. He has two bratvas out for his blood. Backing the man into a corner could make him lash out. There's no telling what he'll do."

"He's earned what's coming to him," I say as Vlad pulls me into his arms. "I regret nothing I did. He sure as hell lost no sleep over hurting me."

"He joined a bratva and got out of jail early." Vlad strokes my hair. "That's impressive. Thanks to you and me, he's lost that forever. His number is up."

The front door bangs and David is there.

"Vladi, you're not gonna fucking believe this," he says."

Vlad lets go of me. "What?"

"The stupid bastard went to Nico, looking for a hiding place. How dumb is that? Nico didn't keep that information to himself, not after Arman scared him so much. He's so desperate to get back into your good books. It's pathetic. He called me while Cassius was there at his house."

I'm shaking. *Please say you got him.*

"What happened?" Vlad asks.

"I told Nico to keep him there and called Sasha, planning on turning up and getting the drop on Cassius, but something went wrong. Nico called me back, gibbering like a moron, and when we arrived, he'd shot Cassius in the face with a shotgun. Hell of a fucking mess."

I feel a stab of vicious glee. Cassius' Jack' Jackson died as he lived—horribly and violently. It couldn't have happened to a more deserving person.

Vlad frowns. "Nico say why he killed him?"

"Cassius was ranting, pacing, waving a gun. He underestimated little Nico, and honestly, so did we. I told him we were simpatico again, but he needed to get his ass out of town for a while. When he calls to confirm he's lying low, I'll transfer the ten million to him, with your permission."

"You don't have Cassius' body? I assume Sasha had no choice but to dispose of him."

"Yeah, he's dealing with it. I grabbed this for you. Thought you might like to have it."

He drops a blood-covered signet ring onto Vlad's outstretched hand. Cassius's ring that cut my lip when he punched me the first time. It feels like forever ago now. A different life. A different *me*.

Vlad presses the ring into my palm.

"Spoils of war, *lisichka*. We win."

I slip it over my middle finger and raise it toward the ceiling. "Fuck yourself, Jack."

Vlad laughs. "Shouldn't you be pointing down? He's not up there." He speaks to David. "Send Nico the cash. He's got the finesse of a herd of elephants, but he did good."

"What are you gonna do now?" David asks.

Vlad grins. "I'm gonna deal with business, *dyadya*. But I need you by my side. Papa gave you a raw deal, and you deserve better. Whaddayasay?"

41

Two hours later…

Cassius

My phone has been ringing non-stop, but I can't shut it off. I'm waiting for David to call me again.

I know what's going on. Most of my acquaintances are chancers, just like me. They wouldn't be calling unless they had something to gain.

Trusov burned me. The fucking cunt. I knew he would piss his pants at the thought of tangling with the Kislev bratva, but it still stings. None of this would have happened if he hadn't sent Hektor to New York.

When my father was laying into my mother, she would scream at him. Tell him abusive bastards like him would get their just desserts. He used to hit me too, but he preferred to fuck with my head.

When I was eight, he upped and left, so I don't know if Mom's prophecy came true, but her constant nagging drove him away. She said they'd been happy before I came along, and as a young kid, that hurt me. When I grew up, I sure as hell made her show me some respect in the way my father taught me. Women learn better when they bruise.

I've done a lot of nasty shit and hurt many people. Deep inside, a tiny voice asks me whether karma is coming for me, too.

The phone rings again from a number I don't recognize. I answer it.

"Yes?"

"How's it going?" David asks.

"After what you told me, I don't dare walk down the fucking street. Ira and Vladimir are buddies now, I take it?"

"They're not fighting. The Trusov and Kislev bratvas have a price on your head. Nice to be wanted, isn't it?"

"Hilarious. Have you done it yet?"

"No. And I'm not going to."

Did he just say that?

"Care to elaborate? We've been through this already. You'll tell Vladimir I'm dead and give him my ring as proof. He'll drop his guard, and you encourage him and Morgana to leave the safety of the city. You point me in their direction. I kill them. The Kislev bratva is yours, and I return to Chicago."

"I'm not doing it." David's voice is resolute. "I was wrong about him. He's not a loose cannon, after all."

I snort. "So?"

"I told Vlad you're dead. It all went as planned—I shot Nico's face off, told Sasha and Vladi his corpse was you, and Sasha disposed of him. As far as anyone else is concerned, Nico left town with a ten-million-dollar bounty payment. I'll give that money to you if you agree to disappear, but I'm out."

I can't fucking believe this.

"Why?"

"When I told Vladi you were dead, I saw something in his face I never saw before. Did he put his woman before his bratva? Yes. But Morgana isn't his weakness. My nephew is in love, and it's given him something to be strong for. She's his greatest asset, and we'll go from strength to strength with her at his side."

What is wrong with this guy? Morgana is *nothing*.

"You think money is enough?" I ask, my voice rising. "I want *respect*. A position in a criminal syndicate. Your nephew got me thrown out of my bratva, and now I'm being hunted by people who should be my subordinates!"

"You'll *never* be bratva." I hear the contempt in David's voice. "Vlad wants to share his responsibilities with me, run our empire as a partnership. It's more than my brother ever did."

"So you're just a coward. Too afraid to seize what's yours."

"You sound like Sergey. Everyone thinks you're dead, you fucking idiot. I did you a solid. Take the money and go. Preferably, to another continent."

Ten million dollars is not chicken feed. But you can't *buy* into a bratva—places are bestowed by birthright, bloodshed or marriage. I did my time, killed in Trusov's name, and was working up to a good relationship with him when fate threw my bitch ex into my path. Even as a ghost, New York and Chicago are off-limits. If someone recognizes me, I'm fucked.

Most would take the money and run.

My father's voice. *You're a weak little bitch, Cass. No one will ever respect you.*

"Okay," I say. "I have little choice. Make a deposit in escrow at JPMorgan, and send me the access code. I'll get out of town."

"*Da.* Then this number will be deactivated, and you'll never hear from me again."

David hangs up. I look out the motel room window and reflect on my future.

I've lost *everything*. No home, no bratva, no job. I thought Trusov respected me, but I was only useful. The moment I became a problem, he tossed me aside just for the approval of another powerful man.

I could buy yachts, houses, whores. But whenever I look in the mirror, I'll see a man who lost his hard-won place in the world just because he didn't kill one red-haired slut when he had the chance.

My father was right. I *am* a little bitch, after all.

42

One week later...

Vlad

I haven't visited the Hamptons property in years, and I'd forgotten how beautiful it was. Sagaponack South has the most luxurious properties in the area, and ours has a spacious beachfront plot to itself. When we were kids, Mama would bring Sasha and me here when Papa's bullshit got too much.

Idiot that I am, I made a promise to my wife. She wanted to start our honeymoon at the beach, just the two of us, before we took my jet to Italy to see her parents. She was desperate to see the beach house, and with Cassius gone and *dyada* David holding the fort, I could deny her no longer.

Morgana loves the place, of course. It smelled kinda musty when we arrived an hour ago, so she lit a candle in the lounge, and just like that, the house was filled with the scent of lemon and lavender.

The candles were Mama's favorites because they reminded her of her home in Tuscany. We have them at our home, too, but my father would never allow them to be lit. One of many things that's gonna change.

I just wish I could kick back and relax.

Morgana and I sit on the edge of the mini pier that links the deck to the beach, our feet in the sand.

"This wine is so good," Morgana says, pulling the bottle from the ice bucket, "but not as good as the view. I can't believe I forgot my camera."

"I'll get you another one tomorrow. If you're gonna be scatter-brained, I'll leave one in every house, every yacht..."

She laughs. "Money really solves everything, doesn't it?"

"No." I wrap my arm around her, pulling her head onto my shoulder. "I can't buy happiness or peace of mind."

Morgana feels me tense up, and she knows what's up. "Are you still brooding over you not getting to kill Cassius yourself?"

"I guess. I wanted to deal with him *my* way."

"Vladi, the outcome would have been exactly the same." The salt breeze whips her auburn hair, and she brushes it away from her face. "You have nothing to prove."

"I'm not so sure. Being here *gets* to me. I love this house—my mother chose everything in it, and I feel her presence here. But this is where I let Lili down. Myself, too."

Morgana winds her fingers around mine. "You act as though you're waiting for your punishment to catch up with you. You've done all you could to atone and didn't even have anything to apologize for." She digs her toes into the sand. "Look at Lili now. Would she have considered auditioning for Juilliard if your father were still alive? The whole family got behind her, brought her out of her shell, and she's like a new person."

My little sister *is* different. My father was like a shadow, blocking the sun and preventing her from growing. Now she's thriving.

My desire to be like my father chafed against my hatred of him. The dissonance left me confused and miserable, and I didn't even know it—the feeling had become part of me. Morgana came into my life and shone her brightness into the darkest places, refusing to accept my insistence that I was a lost cause. She loves me not *despite* my worst aspects but *because* of them. You can't appreciate the highs without knowing what it means to be low. She's seen me at my worst, but not once did she turn her face away.

I laugh as Morgana tries again to take photos with her phone.

"I'm spoiled now." She taps the screen, frowning. "I have an amazing camera that has ten thousand features I don't understand and about twenty I use all the time. This app has six settings and none of them do *anything*."

"*Lisichka*, I think this is a first-world problem, don't you?"

She throws me a glance. "I'm married to a billionaire bratva pakhan. All my problems will be first-world problems now." She flaps her hands in mock hysteria. "Errr nerrr, I want to go opening night at the Op-ear-aaa, but we'll be in the Caribbean. Whatevaaaaa will I dooo?"

"Stop that, you fucking nut," I say, sipping my wine. "You've had too much of this Sancerre or not nearly enough."

Morgana grabs the bottle and swigs from it. "Just remember —*you* dragged my ass into your crazy life. I'll be a dutiful wife in public, but you're getting the real me when it's just us."

"Thank fuck for that." I kiss her forehead. "You're stuck with the real *me*, too, so fair's fair."

She squares up the shot one more time and clicks the button, capturing the sunset perfectly. "There. I'll send this one to Lili. She wants to come out here soon."

"That'll be good," I say, snatching her phone, "but she's not here now."

Morgana lunges at me, trying to grab it, but I skim it along the deck and out of reach.

"We're still doing that, huh?" She folds her arms and pouts in the petulant manner I love so much.

"You convinced me to deactivate the tracking app, but I still reserve the right to toss the stupid thing if it's taking your attention from me."

She rolls her eyes. "*So* dramatic. You have my attention now. Entertain me."

"I intend to."

I pick her up and throw her over my shoulder, and she giggles, hitting my back with her fists. "Put me down, you big nasty bratva man! I don't love you, I don't enjoy being your wife, and I definitely won't *ever* have sex with you!"

"On all three counts, *lisichka*, you're a liar."

I carry her into the house and drop her on the bed. She squeals and tries to roll away, but I'm faster and stronger. I pin her under me, tugging her sundress over her hips as I sink my teeth into her neck.

"There's no one to hear you," I say. "I can make you scream as much as I like."

"You don't care who hears anyway," she says, turning her head to catch my lips. "You're an inconsiderate asshole."

She likes to insult me. Usually, when she wants me riled up and ready to get nasty with her, which is more often than I expected.

"You're a good girl, Morgana, but you should watch your mouth before I shove something in it to shut you up."

"Breadsticks?" She nips my earlobe. "Potpourri?"

That does it.

I sit back on my heels and free my cock, catching it in my hand as it springs free. Morgana's mouth falls open as she stares.

"That's the posture I want," I say. "Now, put those pretty lips around my cock."

I get to my feet, and she sits at the edge of the bed, her warm mouth at the perfect height. My hands sink into her hair, and I sigh as her tongue slides over my swollen tip. I allow her to tease me for a minute, but it's not long before I'm panting, throbbing with the need for more.

"If you keep that up, I'm gonna have to fuck your face."

She looks up at me and bats her eyelashes. "That would be horrible." She laps at me again and smiles. "I wouldn't want *that*."

I growl and let go of my cock to get a better grip on her head. With both hands holding her, there's nothing she can do to stop me.

"Put your hands under your legs, and don't move them," I say, bouncing my cock on her chin. "Now open up and take it."

I slip my cock over her tongue. Her throat ripples against me as she relaxes her muscles, suppressing the reflex, but I can push further than that. *A little more...*

A primal pleasure surges through me as I hit the limit. She gags hard, coating me in the thick, slippery saliva that is the hallmark of a deep throat.

"Fuck *me*, that's hot," I say. I withdraw, marveling at the sight of my glistening cock. Morgana gasps as I slap my wet shaft on her cheek.

"More, *lisichka*." I slide into her mouth and thrust, holding her head so she has to take me. I bottom out roughly, and she gives a strangled cry.

My wife loves it when I use her. I love it when she uses *me*. I'm sure my associates see her bruised neck and assume I'm an abusive bastard, but anyone who knows me and Morgana can see I'm a fucking simp for my wife. She's gagging on my cock now because *she* wants it as much as I do.

I fuck her mouth with firm jerks of my hips, enjoying the feel of her tongue lashing at the head as I move. I'm tempted to shoot my load straight into her willing mouth, but I must resist. Her pussy is waiting for me, and if she doesn't get what she wants, I'll be in trouble.

With some difficulty, I yank my cock out of her mouth and release her head.

"What do you want?" I say. "Just ask, and I'll give it to you."

Morgana wipes her lips with the back of her hand. To my surprise, she grasps my slick cock in her hand and starts jerking it slowly.

"Look at me," she says.

I stare at her, hypnotized by her amber eyes as they burn into mine. Isn't it *me* who's supposed to say that?

I tower over her, muscles shimmering with perspiration, raging cock pulsating with ecstasy as she works me over. She may be at my feet now, her hair wild and her throat sore, but I'm entirely at her mercy. And there's nowhere I'd rather be.

"What *I* want is simple." Morgana pumps her hand slowly, and I groan. "I want you to take me to the kitchen, sit me on the island, and eat my pussy until I'm on the brink. Then you can rail me however you like, but I want a mess, Vladi. When we're done, I want that kitchen floor to be a health code violation."

I'd laugh if I weren't losing my mind. *Fucking hell.* I love how much she wants me. It's a novel experience to fuck someone I love and respect. Who knew it could be so good?

43

Morgana

I'm always impressed at how easily Vlad can toss me around. He picks me up like I'm nothing and carries me to the kitchen as ordered, sitting me on my feet beside the island. His cock nestles between my thighs as he leans in to kiss me.

"You taste of me," he says, licking his lips. "I like that." He slips his fingers under the elastic of my panties, pulling them off. "Now turn around and bend over the island. Hold on to the other side."

I love the feel of the thin cotton dress against my bare ass. I assume the position, and he slides the dress up, exposing me to his gaze. He reaches between my legs and taps my thigh.

"Wider, *lisichka*." He picks up my right leg, resting my knee on the counter. "Keep this up here."

The kitchen window is open, and I feel the breeze on my hot pussy. I didn't know how much I needed him inside me until he opened me up like that, but now I feel desperately empty.

"This little pussy is beautiful," Vlad murmurs. "So pink and wet. I love fucking it." He rubs my asshole, making me flinch.

His dirty words wash over me like a spell. I didn't know men like him existed. Men who love to fuck, who love to talk about how they're gonna do it. If this is the upside of being married to a dangerous guy like Vladi, it's worth it.

"Please touch me." I wiggle my hips. "I'm such a slut for you. All you had to do was fuck my face, and I'm soaked. I can't wait to be full of your come."

Vlad's face is close to my pussy, and I feel him exhale heavily at my words.

He's gotten very into the idea of us having a baby. Although my pill hasn't worn off yet, my husband has surprised us both by developing something of a breeding kink. The sheer amount of come he's unloaded into me this last week alone has been incredible. The man wants me to leak his seed every minute of the day.

"Oh, you can fucking count on it," he says. He thrusts two fingers deep into my pussy, and I cry out, the fullness easing the ache inside. "I'm gonna wreck your little cunt first, though." He reaches around to my face with his free hands, his fingers rubbing my lips. "Get on these."

I open my mouth, and he shoves his fingers deep. I feel them smash into the tender spot his cock made only minutes ago, and I cough, hocking onto his hand.

"Perfect." He withdraws and rubs the saliva onto my rosy asshole, opening it up as his fingers pump my pussy. "Touch your clit while I do this."

I slip my hand under my body and find my clit. It's unbelievably sensitive, and the slightest swipe of my fingertip sends bolts of molten bliss up my spine. I rest my cheek on the cold marble and moan as Vlad finger-fucks me, the firm motion complimenting my own touch.

Vlad pulls his hands away, and I yelp with loss before I realize he's getting comfortable. With one hand, he grips my thigh, holding my knee up and high. The leg still on the ground is cramping, but his support removes the pressure. I cry out as he inserts his index finger into my asshole, adding the other three fingers to my pussy.

"I love stuffing you," he says. "It looks phenomenal. Do you feel good, baby?"

"Yes," I gasp. "Make me come. Keep doing that, and I'll squirt everywhere."

With a slight turn of his wrist and a curl of his fingers, he finds the right spot, and my eyes roll.

"I know." He speeds up, pinning my leg to the counter to keep me in place. "What do you think I'm trying to do? Don't you dare let up on that slutty clit. Be a good girl, and come for me now."

I'm already gone. I'm reduced to the sensations in my core, and I scream as my climax smashes through me. My pussy floods, wetness flowing down my leg, but Vlad keeps going, thrusting his fingers in and out of me as I clench and quiver around them. My voice drops to a whimper, and he pulls his hand free.

"Don't catch your breath," he says. He hauls me to my feet and spins me around, pushing me face-first onto the couch. "I'm gonna pound that sweet little pussy. You can take it, right?"

Vlad doesn't need an answer. He knows I can.

He kneels behind me, grabs my hips, and pulls me onto my knees. I spread my legs wide, my ass in the air, my head on the couch cushion.

"You're all puffy," he says, sounding awestruck. "The only way you could look sexier is with my come dripping out of you."

"So get on with it."

He winds my hair into a thick rope, wrapping it around his palm. His cock is slippery between my legs, and he grasps my hip as he nudges into my pussy.

"You ready for me?" He slips a little deeper, and I hiss through my teeth. Even after all his attention, his girth still knocks the wind out of me every time. "Because I'm gonna slam you like you're my slut, not the love of my life."

"I'm both," I say as he fills me. "Give it to me."

Vlad wasn't joking. He finds his stride instantly, forging in and out of me, and I have to pant to handle the onslaught. My clit is a bundle of overwrought nerves, but when I touch it, I don't want to stop.

"I won't come until you give me another," Vlad says, his breathing ragged. He pulls my hair. "Tell me how much you want my come."

"I want it! I want your come, Vladi!"

"I want *yours* first." He slaps my ass. "Scream for me, *lisichka*."

My clit is verging on soreness, but I can push through it. I grit my teeth as he bottoms out hard inside me, and it's all I need. I give a tortured howl as my second orgasm pulsates in my core, making my internal walls ripple and spasm on Vlad's thick shaft. He pushes me onto my stomach and grunts as he empties into my body, his come overflowing and mingling with mine as it pools beneath us.

For a few minutes, I can't even feel my legs. There's only my husband's breathing, heavy and hot. Before long, I begin to feel a chill and nudge him.

"Come and get in bed with me," he says, climbing off me. "But show me what I wanna see first."

I get to my feet, tugging my dress down as I walk away. I look almost respectable for a second, but I know what my man wants. Lifting my skirt to my waist, I bend at the hips and look at Vlad between my legs. A little squeeze and I feel his come running down my swollen pussy lips. It drips onto the floor between my feet.

Vlad kneels and scoops the come onto his finger. He parts my pussy lips with his other hand and pushes his seed back inside me.

He leans between my thighs to kiss me. "Hang onto that, baby. You never know."

Vlad runs his fingers lightly down my spine, the rhythmic movement calming my racing heart. Ever since we first met, he's been able to soothe me, and since he's been sleeping at my side, I've had no more nightmares. Even when Cassius returned to my life, Vlad's presence overwhelmed the traumatic memories and crowded them out.

I didn't believe in love. Not really. Or at least, I didn't think it was meant for *me*. I sometimes wonder if Vlad's mother felt the same way, but then I remember she had a man she adored, only to lose him. She was forced to abandon everything that mattered to her and start again in a life that must have been worse than hell. The woman was a warrior, and her husband feared her quiet fortitude and steadfast sense of hope.

Sergey didn't die alone, but he died lonely. All the pain and suffering he wrought upon his family amounted to nothing.

It comes to me in a moment of inspiration—Sergey was desperately jealous of his son. Vlad had his mother's love, which was more potent than the most brutal of beatings and more enduring than any generational legacy of abuse. The old man knew his oldest son would dump the weight of his father's expectations and embrace love if only he had the chance. So he tried to remove that opportunity by forcing marriage upon him.

How ironic. Had Sergey not forced Vlad's hand, we would never have found our way to each other's hearts.

I roll onto my side, ready to share my insight with my husband. He's dozing, a sweet smile playing on his lips, and

I decide not to trouble him with these heavy thoughts. It's too good to see him at peace.

I put my lips to the shell of his ear. "Vladi, I'm gonna go get us some burgers."

He grins, his eyes still closed. "Good idea. But this is the Hamptons. Don't go looking for a McDonald's."

"I saw a Brazilian place on the way in, near the riding club. They'll have what I want."

"They'll deliver, *lisichka*. Just call them."

"I fancy a walk, you lazy ass." I slap him on the shoulder. "No one's forcing you to come with."

It'll take around fifteen minutes to get to the restaurant, and it's not yet dark. The beachfront is quiet, and I want to get a few more good shots of the sea as the light fades.

"Alright, *moya zhena*." He waves his hand. "Take my black Amex—they'll piss their pants with joy when they see it. If you want dodo paté or a rack of dinosaur ribs, they'll get them."

I laugh. "Who are we, The Flintstones?"

He opens one eye. "The *who*?"

"*Jesus.* You've never seen—right." I get to my feet, pulling on my sundress. "To be continued. I'm gonna pick up the food and more wine, and we are gonna watch the greatest animated series ever made."

Vlad gives me a sleepy nod. "*Da, komandir.*"

44

Vlad

A squealing sound. It's my ears ringing. They did that when my father hit my head, and tinnitus still comes and goes, even now.

No, it's something else. My ringtone.

I sit up, blinking. I pull on my boxers and rummage around in my clothes, finding my phone in my pants pocket.

"Sasha, *brat*. You miss me already?"

Just the way he's breathing makes me realize something is seriously wrong.

Vladi, Lilyana, she—" Sasha swallows. He's barely keeping it together. "—Lili went to Juilliard alone. She lied about when the audition was. Maybe she didn't want them to think she was weird or couldn't handle it, I don't know. But someone followed her, and when she came out..."

No. No, not Lilyana. I want to stay in this moment and not have to know.

I've never known Sasha to cry. Even at Mama's funeral, he went off alone and returned with red-rimmed eyes, hiding behind his jokes.

"Tell me."

"Five of her fingers are broken," Sasha says, his voice cracking. "Her collarbone, her wrist. Her face—oh Jesus *fuck*, Vladi. I'm so glad you're not here. If you saw her, you'd die. Whoever beat her really fucked her up."

I slump to the ground, leaning against the door. "Is she conscious? Where is she now?"

"You'd be proud of her." Sasha sniffs, trying to compose himself. "She's in the hospital, under sedation. Avel, Arman, and I are with her. She's only alive at all because someone found her in an alleyway. Her tracker got broken in the attack."

I can't think of anyone who'd go so low. Lilyana is entirely innocent. She's not involved in the business and has no information worth knowing; there's no reason to imagine she would. Someone intended this attack to send a message.

"Where's David?" I say. "What does he think about this?"

"He *was* here. He took one look at Lili and left. Maybe he has a lead, maybe not, but I'm worried about him. He's not picking up his phone."

A chill seeps into my bones.

I've been restless and unable to calm my mind since Cassius's death. Something wasn't right, and I knew it. It was like an itch I couldn't scratch. Although Trusov backed off and closed the matter, I couldn't let it go.

Loving Morgana was something I never dreamed of. I didn't think love would find me or I'd be capable of feeling it.

For the first time, I saw the best in everything and everyone. I truly believed Lili was ready to spread her wings and fly. And *dyadya* David shifted from an undermining, malevolent influence to the father figure I wanted so badly. When Papa died, I tried to scrub him out, and bringing David closer to the bratva and giving him some control was my way of doing that.

But now Lili is broken and bleeding. And where is David?

Come to think of it, where the fuck is *Morgana*? I have no idea how long I was asleep.

"The nurse said Lili was conscious when she got to the hospital," Sasha says. "She wasn't coherent, but she kept saying something over and over."

"What was it?"

"She said, 'I didn't tell him.'"

Sweet Jesus. What the *fuck*?

"Please, Sasha, stay with Lili. I'll be back as soon as possible."

"*Da*. Hurry. I'll keep trying David."

I hang up and call Morgana. *Come on, lisichka. Pick up. We have to get out of here.*

You have reached the voice mailbox of—

I swipe the call away and try again, panic heavy in my chest. I draw a deep breath, trying to relieve the tightness gripping my lungs.

You have reached the voice mailbox of Morgana—

Don't do this to me. I don't know who I'm talking to, but I'm saying it aloud. God, The Devil—fuck it, any deity or demon can come to my aid, and I'll let Him eat my soul, but don't let the ones I love pay for my sinful life.

I call her once more. After two rings, she picks up.

"Vladi?"

"Morgana! Where are you? We gotta—"

A short scream, and the line cuts out.

I drop the phone and collapse onto my back, digging my hands into my scalp as my roar of anguish shakes the house.

I scramble to my feet and dress quickly before running out of the property and onto the road.

I have to find my wife.

45

Morgana

My phone vanishes from my hand, and for an insane moment, I think it's Vlad playing a prank on me. Before I can turn around, an arm wraps my shoulders tightly, and I understand I'm in trouble.

I pedal my feet, trying to find the ground, but it's useless. I'm being dragged back along the path toward the beach, and my assailant is far stronger than me.

"Let go!" I cry, elbowing the man in the gut. Something glints in my eye line, and the flat of a blade chills the skin of my neck.

"You are such a whore," a voice hisses. "Look at these bruises. You had the nerve to go whining to the cops when I hurt you, but you'll let some Cossack prick do the same and pretend to love it just because he's rich?"

I'm going crazy. This can't be happening.

Cassius Jackson is back from the dead.

"Jack? Stop." I force myself to stay still, my pulse throbbing against the firmness of the metal at my throat. His other arm is hooked around me, pinning my body to his. "Don't do this. You don't have to hurt me."

"You sound just like you always did, Morgana. Begging, whining. It never worked, did it? This is your problem. You *never* fucking learn."

How is he alive? I have his signet ring. David saw his body, and Sasha cleaned up the mess. What the hell is going on?

"Why did you come back?"

"Because you and your husband ruined my life." He's walking me fast in front of him, the knife cutting tiny slivers of pain into my tender throat. "I told you so many times. I deserve to *be* somebody. And I was right on track until I was sent to find a murderer. You turned out to be his fucking wife, and as soon as you recognized me, I knew I was screwed." He kicks me hard in the shin, and I almost buckle to the ground, but he hauls me up again. "But I'm here now, aren't I? Because I'm *strong*."

Ah. This is familiar.

Cassius's biggest fear is that he's weak. His father said he was a pussy, a piece of shit, feeble, puny. Cassius would recount this when he was drunk and melancholy, but I always knew where it was headed. Eventually, he would realize he'd said too much, feel stupid for revealing his messed-up inner landscape, and beat me to a pulp as punishment for 'making him feel bad.'

I told Vlad all about it. Weirdly, he said he could relate to it as his father had been much the same. But Vlad had his Mama, and her love cut through all that. Who could Cassius have been if he'd been shown some kindness as a kid? Even after his father left, his mother was a bitter, vicious woman who projected all her shortcomings onto her son. By the time he grew up and turned his fists on her, he had known nothing but rejection.

When I first got to know Cassius, my heart wept for his pain. When Vlad forced himself into my life, I thought I was making the same mistake. Thank God I found the courage to look beyond the surface despite my fear.

"You *are* strong," I say, my voice strained as I try not to flex my throat. "You've been through a lot and are a victim of circumstance here. Don't make it worse for yourself."

Cassius snorts a laugh. "You know what? I was gonna kill you and your idiot husband, but I think I might take you back to Chicago with me. I already beat that pea-brained Kislev girl to a pulp, and I could go back any time for her or your little slut friend. So you'd have an incentive to behave for me."

Tears pour down my cheeks. "You bastard. Did you make Lilyana tell you where we were?"

"I didn't need to. She's brave or dumb, but she wouldn't give you up, no matter how many backhands I gave her. Remember those, Morgana? But she had her phone, with a nice shiny notification on the lock screen from you. She was out cold, so I unlocked her screen with one of her broken fingers and saw the picture you sent." I hear the mirth in his voice. "It was a pleasant drive down here, and I soon found the place. People were real helpful when I asked."

"We were told you were dead," I say. "How can that be?"

"Vladimir's uncle David was all set to betray him, but he changed his mind. I was gonna run with the money, but I couldn't bear to let you get away with fucking me over. With the whole city looking for me, it was safest to stay near the Kislev house—the last place anyone would look. I took an apartment nearby and kept watch, and when I saw Lilyana go out alone, I knew that was my chance."

"You didn't have the balls to take on any of the men, did you?"

Cassius's arm around my neck grows tighter. "Fuck yourself, you cunt. I'm here now, aren't I? And where is he, huh? Your hero is *nowhere*. I could slit your throat and leave you to bleed out right here, and he'd never know it was me. But that'd be too easy. I need *him* too."

I see the house ahead, but the lights are off even though it's now dark. Vlad must be out looking for me. I wonder if he knows about Lili, and the thought of her sets me off crying again. What if she's dead?

As we approach, I see Vlad's car is gone. Cassius shoves me up the steps and smashes the glass panel in the door with the knife handle. He reaches through and unlocks the door.

"Keep your mouth shut," he says. He takes my phone from his pocket. "Let's give loverboy a call."

46

Vlad

I'm parked on Sagg Street, staring along the road. It wasn't until I was driving that I remembered I'd taken the one gun I brought with me into the house, so I'm not even fucking armed.

Morgana could have been anywhere, and I expected to see her toting a takeout bag and complaining about the lack of cell phone reception. I asked some people, but no one had seen her en route.

I'm struggling to drag the air into my lungs, which burn with the exertion. My phone is on the passenger seat, and as I will it to ring, it lights up. I grab it and swipe to green.

"Morgana, is that you?"

"Vladi."

"David?" I squeeze the phone, wanting to hurl it out the window. Every second I spend talking to him is a second where Morgana can't reach me. "What the fuck is going on?"

David sighs deeply but doesn't reply. The silence lasts too long.

"What did you do?"

"I fucked up, Vladi." David sounds old and so much like my father. It's like hearing his voice from beyond the grave. "I thought you would be a lame duck and lead our bratva to ruin. At least, that's what I told myself. Your father and grandfather led me to believe the only way to get what I wanted was by force. When Sergey died, I felt like it was my right to control the bratva. I may not have been groomed to lead, but it doesn't mean I didn't deserve a chance."

"Cassius isn't dead, is he?" I yell. "You spun me a fucking lie and sent the bastard after me when my guard was down."

"I was going to, but I didn't. Cassius wanted you dead, but I paid him off instead. You gave me a share and treated me like an equal, Vladi. I had never experienced that before, and I never expected it. I'm sorry. You're not your Papa, and it's a damn good thing."

"There's nothing you can fucking say now. You know that, right? Lilyana is in the hospital, and my wife is missing." I can no longer restrain myself, and my words drip with rage. "David. Where the *fuck* is my wife?"

"I don't know. But it may be too late. I saw Lilyana lying in that hospital bed and realized what I'd done. I couldn't take it back. I really thought he'd take the money and go..."

David says nothing more. I hear a rustling sound like he's setting the phone down somewhere.

"David?"

A gunshot from the other end of the line.

The treacherous piece of shit took himself out rather than face the music. *Of course.*

I turn the car around and head back to the house. Maybe Morgana is there, and if she isn't, I have no doubt Cassius will show up looking for me.

The phone rings again, and Morgana's number appears on the screen. I answer it, certain it's Cassius calling to gloat.

"Where is my wife? If you've harmed a hair on her head, I swear to God I'll—"

"It's me," Morgana says, her voice hoarse. She sounds like she's been crying forever. "I'm okay, Vladi. Please don't shout."

"Holy shit," I say, my voice breaking from sheer relief. "I never thought I'd hear your voice again. God help me, *lisichka*. I nearly lost my mind."

"You don't have any back-up," she whispers. "You're alone out here. Just *go*."

"Never." The very thought makes me sick with anger. "I'm your husband. I swore to protect you. This is my fault." I punch the steering wheel hard. "But know this. That fucker will wish for hell long before I send him there."

A muffled sound, then Cassius's voice, loud in the speaker. "Vladimir motherfucking Kislev! How's tricks," he adopts a sarcastic tone, "*tovarishch*?"

"You had money," I say. "A chance to start again. Still, you came after us. Why?"

"I wanted to go back to Trusov. I knew you wouldn't let it happen—*you* wanted me dead. So don't give me that shit. You set this entire chain of events in motion. *You* murdered Hektor and Serra. You're the one who insisted on tracking me down to avenge Morgana. And *you* threatened Trusov, putting me in a position where I was fighting for my life. What did you *think* I would do? I'm smart. Strong."

Morgana told me he's terrified of appearing weak. Does he think abducting one defenseless woman makes him look powerful?

"Yeah, you fucking bet." I'm approaching the long drive to the house, and I switch off the car's headlamps, slowing to a crawl. "I'm guessing you don't have your own Hamptons home-from-home. I assume you've helped yourself to mine?"

"Yep." Cassius cackles and I realize he's losing it. "Better hurry if you want to say goodbye."

～

The glass in the front door is broken, and the door is ajar. I pick my way through the shards as I enter the hallway.

"Cassius!" I shout. "Let's talk about it."

Silence. Morgana is already dead, or he's keeping her quiet. If he hurt her, I don't know what I'd l do. What's worse than death? I'd have to make him suffer in every imaginable way before I sent him into eternity's merciless clutches.

My gun is under the bed upstairs, where I can reach it easily at night. The house isn't huge, and it's mostly open plan, but it's now dark, and there are still plenty of places to hide.

So when I enter the lounge, it's a shock to see Cassius standing there, a long blade at Morgana's throat. The candle Morgana lit earlier is still burning on the table, and shadows flicker on the wall.

"Let's find out if you love her, shall we?" he sneers.

I look at my wife. Her face is streaked with tears, but her eyes are aflame, and I see blood running down her neck. For a sick moment, I think he's slashed her throat, but when I look again, I realize the cuts are superficial. For now.

"Of course I love her." I take a step back and raise my hands. "I'll call it off, Cassius. Just let her go. Her life for yours."

"I'm already dead, remember? Why should I accept any assurances from you?" He grips Morgana tightly, drawing a gasp from her. "And besides, whether I leave here or die, I'm taking Morgana with me. You don't deserve a happy ending, nor does a slut like her." He grins at me. "Surely the pakhan of the Kislev bratva can do better than my sloppy seconds?"

I clench my fists.

"I'll go with him." Morgana's voice is small and resigned. "Don't risk fighting for me. Go home to your family, Vladi. They need you."

"*Lisichka*, I can't do that. *I* need *you*."

"Oh, this is fucking pathetic," Cassius says, laughing. "Isn't love grand? All it got you was a whore wife and a bratva that's crumbling under the weight of your failure. Was it worth it?"

I hold Morgana's gaze but speak to Cassius. "Yes. A weak man like you wouldn't understand."

47

Morgana

Whatever Cassius's plan was when he showed up here, he didn't think it through. Maybe he thought Vlad would panic or capitulate to save my life, and he could enjoy having the upper hand before killing Vlad and stealing me away. Does he think the rest of the Kislevs would take that outcome lying down? That Trusov, terrified and eager to please, wouldn't hand him over at the first opportunity?

"This won't work, Cassius," I say. "Don't do this."

He isn't listening to me. His body is tense, and his hand shakes, quivering the blade against my skin. I lean away from it, but he doesn't notice.

I see what's up.

I told my husband all about my vicious ex and his insecurities. Cassius's festering fears drove him to abuse me, trying to prove to himself that he was the powerful one.

Vlad can see Cassius is unraveling. Making him angry enough to lose control is a risky strategy but the best chance we have. I'm afraid but somehow calm, and I look at Vlad, telling him with my eyes.

Do it. Make him mad. Tear at that psychological wound until the bastard can't take it anymore.

"If you weren't such a pussy," Vlad says, "you'd have more respect. Ira Trusov would value you more. He didn't even *try* to fight for you."

Cassius growls under his breath. He presses the knife against me, cutting me anew, but he's not focused on me. He's fixated on Vlad.

Vlad steps closer, and I understand what he's doing. If he puts himself within reach of Cassius's arm, he might lash out at him with the knife, giving me a chance to escape.

I blink away tears. *Oh, God, please.* Don't let Vlad die defending me.

"Your father knew, didn't he, Cassius?" Vlad smiles, and Cassius flinches. "He said as much. That you wouldn't have the strength to do what's necessary. I think he was right."

My husband's features twist into an ugly sneer, chilling me to the bone. He's channeling his father now, putting Sergey's bile and vitriolic disgust behind every word. He even *looks* like him.

We measure the space between life and death in moments. Any second, Cassius could spring to action and slit my throat. He could plunge the blade into Vlad's chest. Nothing is stopping him. Yet he stares at Vlad, paralyzed by the words he heard so many times when he was a helpless child.

"Is that why your dad left?" Vlad edges nearer. "He couldn't bear to look at his weak, scrawny kid anymore? You got in the gym since then, but it's not enough. Did you really think you could command respect in a bratva? You couldn't even keep control of Morgana. She got you thrown in fucking jail." He grins. "Now *that's* pathetic. Did the other cons fuck you? They usually know a little bitch when they see one."

Cassius throws me to the ground, and I hit my head on the table, sending the still-lit candle rolling across the carpet. He hurls himself at Vlad, but he's not quick enough, and as Vlad moves aside, Cassius loses his balance. He plunges his blade into Vlad's thigh as he falls.

"Vladi!" I try to get to my feet, but my head is swimming. I grab Cassius's ankle and sink my teeth into his shin, and he kicks me in the face with his other foot, dropping his knife. Vlad reaches for the blade, but Cassius stamps on his injured leg and gets to it first.

"Get the gun, Morgana!" Vlad cries. "You know where it is! Run and get it!"

I'm on my feet, my head pounding. The room is brightening, and in a detached way, I'm aware of heat as the drapes catch alight, flames licking toward the ceiling.

Vlad is still yelling, but I can't hear him anymore. All the sounds have faded to a peaceful, droning static.

Stay awake, Morgana. Stay alive!

Cassius is moving toward me fast, the knife in his hand. I spin and run for the stairs.

The gun is under the bed the gun is under the bed the gun is under the bed—

He's on my heels, snatching at my legs. I wait until I reach the landing before slamming my elbow behind me at head height, hoping for the best. The bone connects with Cassius's nose, and he roars as he falls back down the stairwell.

I scramble down the passage toward the bedroom, pinballing off the walls. My legs graze on the carpet as I grab the gun under the bed. When I emerge, Cassius is framed in the doorway, growing larger as he races toward me.

"You're gonna die, you little bitch!"

A bolt of adrenaline fires through my body, powering my limbs, and I slam the door in Cassius's face. He smashes his shoulder into it as I slide the deadbolt. I lean on the door, holding it closed, and he slams his shoulder into it again and again, the wood splintering more with each impact. I whimper, tears running down my cheeks.

"Let me in, bitch! I shoulda just murdered you before you fucked me over. How many times you gotta ruin my life?"

He's gonna kill me. Just like I always feared he would.

I'm panicking, the edges of my vision growing fuzzy as I struggle to breathe. I can't hold this door shut for long. He's stronger than I am. The gun is in my hand, but I can barely see.

Slam. I brace my legs, trying to stay on my feet. Tears run down my cheeks.

"I'll show your precious head to Vlad before I kill him, shall I? Or is he burning?"

What did Vlad tell me to do?

Slam. My back bounces off the door.

Take the safety off. My fingers shake as I fumble for the switch, but I can't find it.

Slam. Slam. Slam.

Wait. It's Vlad's Glock. It doesn't have a safety switch.

"You're fucking dead, Morgana!"

Smoke billows past the window outside. I *have* to do this. It'll only take one more good barge to smash this door, and I must be ready.

I leap away from the door, twisting as I fall to the ground. The battered wood buckles and Cassius is in the room. I wheel around and level the pistol at his chest as he barrels toward me.

With a scream, I squeeze the trigger. Six shots at close range, one after the other. Bullets thump into Cassius's chest, and he spins, crumpling against the wall. I watch him for a moment, positive he'll get up again, but he's gone.

The shrill whine in my ears gives way to a deafening roar. It can't be more than a minute since I ran out of the lounge, but it feels like hours ago. Is the whole place on fire?

I have to find Vladi.

My legs don't want to carry me, but I force them to move. As I round the corner onto the stairwell, smoke billows into my face, acrid and sour, and I duck, trying to get below it. I see Vlad at the bottom, crawling. His pants are soaked in blood, his face ashen. I half-run, half-fall down the stairs, dropping to my knees beside him.

"I shot him, Vladi." I get my arm under him, but he's too heavy. "Come on. Get up."

"I've killed so many people," he whispers. "but when he put a knife to your throat, I felt like the world was ending. I was so afraid." He coughs. "But not anymore, because you're gonna be okay. Get out of here. You have my money and my family. You'll be fine."

"No!" I try again to lift him. "We have a life to live. *Together*." I punch him in the shoulder. "You don't get to make me love you only to leave me on my own! If you die now, I'll never forgive you!"

Vlad gets to his feet, leaning heavily on me. My knees are on the verge of buckling.

"Through the kitchen," he croaks. "The patio doors."

The kitchen is already burning but just about passable. I gasp at the heat, my skin stinging as we make for the doors that lead onto the deck.

A few more steps. Just a few more.

48

Vlad

I roll onto my side, trying to focus. My eyes are hot from the fire, and I blink rapidly to stop them from drying out.

The dry, salt-burnished wood of the house didn't stand a chance. The whole place is an inferno. Nothing and no one could possibly survive.

Cassius is in there, riddled with bullets. There's no way he walked out of that building. But I don't know what happened to Morgana. After she shot Cassius and ran to me, things got hazy.

She helped me to my feet, and we made it out onto the deck. Or was it just *me* who made it? I remember falling on the sand and rolling onto my back as the rain started. Now it's lashing down in sheets, and I'm soaked to the skin.

I took such an appalling risk, baiting Cassius like that. If he'd slit Morgana's throat there and then, I'd never have forgiven myself. But even as he raved and screamed, I knew. He'd been kicked down his whole life, knowing only the aggression and brutality he brought to bear as an adult. He was profoundly afraid to feel anything but rage and entitlement—if the mask cracked, the pain might hit him again. The gnawing thought that maybe his father was right. That's how I knew I could break him without laying a finger on him.

Cassius Jackson was the man *I* could have been.

I haul myself onto my feet but collapse to my knees, feeble as a kitten. The sand beneath me is soaked in my blood.

If Morgana is in there, burning, I'll lie down and die. But while there's a chance she's alive, I have to try.

Lights on the drive. Headlamps.

I don't care who it is as long as they save Morgana. I could be arrested, tortured, or murdered. I don't give a shit. But let my love survive.

My feet feel like blocks of concrete. I slide them through the sand, barely lifting them as I walk. My vision is blurry, but I can see two figures approaching me.

"Vladi!"

I've never been happier to see Sasha. He hurls himself under my arm, supporting me, as Arman takes the other side.

"No," I say, my voice a painful rasp. "Morgana. Find my wife."

Sasha leans my weight onto Arman, and then he's away, running to the side of the house. I hear him yelling her name.

"Sasha," I say. "Find her."

"Take it easy, *bratan*," Arman says. "Is that cunt Cassius in there?"

"Shot."

"You sure? Because I swear if the fucker isn't dead this time—"

"He's dead."

Fire trucks are pulling up, lights flashing everywhere. Arman dumps me in the back of an ambulance, and a paramedic presses a patch of gauze to my thigh.

A firefighter is yelling in my face. "Anyone in there? Mr. Kislev! Is there anyone in the house?"

I look over his shoulder. My brother walks toward us, silhouetted against the backlit smoke and steam.

He has a body draped over his arms.

The paramedic pushes me aside and runs to assist Sasha. They put Morgana on the gurney beside me, an oxygen mask over her face. She's blackened from smoke, her hair greasy and streaked with soot. Her face is shiny like she's sunburned. She's unconscious.

The paramedic slams the ambulance doors and dives into the driver's seat. I take my wife's hand and press her wrist to my cheek, feeling her pulse fluttering like a bird.

"You're so fucking brave, *lisichka*. Hang on in there. You're gonna be alright."

∼

Eighteen hours later...

"Morgana will recover fully within a few days. She may suffer from shortness of breath for a while, but it all looked worse than it was. It was more shock and fright than anything."

"Good," I say, my tone brusque.

This doctor is getting on my nerves. He tends to talk to me and not to my wife, as though I'm in charge of her. Doesn't he know she saved my life *and* her own?

"Thank you, doctor," Morgana says. She waits until he's gone before speaking to me. "Don't be rude, Vladi. I'm okay, and so are you."

The wound in my leg is deep and pretty fucking painful. It missed the artery by an inch but could have been a different story. I needed a lot of stitches and a blood transfusion to get me right again.

Morgana got me out of the house just as the fire took hold, but her legs gave out, and she fell, dropping me on the deck. She rolled off onto the sand, and that's the last she knew before she came round in the ambulance.

I've never known joy like when I saw her beautiful eyes again. They rested on my face, and as she smiled, I knew it was all over. We'd made it.

I told Sasha and Arman the whole tale, and then they went home at my insistence, to be with Lilyana. Arman found David's car in the hospital parking lot, the old man's brain splattered over the seat. It only took one amoral mortuary assistant and a wedge of cash to get that dealt with, and our usual people hauled the car away. I'm unsure what cover story we'll tell, but it's not my priority.

I'm only two hours from the city, but I wanted things locked down quickly. Sasha surprised me by jumping straight into action, calling in favors to shore up our defenses and quell the rumor mill ahead of my return to Manhattan. Threats and bribes work best when used together—like I told Morgana, it's the carrot-and-stick thing.

Morgana flexes her neck. "It aches a bit still," she says, touching the dressing on her wounds. She stretches in her chair and yawns. "I hate hospitals."

"We'll leave as soon as Sasha and Arman can come back together. One of them needs to drive my car home."

"You're supposed to be resting for a couple of days. The doctor won't like it."

"*Lisichka*, I'm not staying here and paying Michelin prices for the swill they call food. I need Dulcie's cooking and my own bed with my wife in it."

"But we never got the burgers," she says, smiling.

The humor doesn't last. She looks away, her pretty face marred with pain, and I take her hand.

"You did what you had to, Morgana. Cassius could have backed down, but he didn't. You wanted to live. You wanted *me* to live. What choice did you have?"

"This is the bratva." She glances at me. "Kill or be killed. Dominate or be dominated. Right?"

"Sometimes. But not everything is that way. Maybe we can find beauty amid all the nasty shit."

She grins. "But keep some of *your* nasty. I'd hate for you to lose your edge."

I kiss her palm, then bite the tip of her thumb. "My love, you *sharpen* my edges, not dull them. Believe me, I've got all the rough you could ever want."

EPILOGUE

One month later...

Morgana

I hug Josie for the tenth time. "You've got everything, right? Panties, Tylenol, condoms?"

"In that order? I'm going traveling. On *Earth*. There will be stores, you know."

"I just wish you'd tell me what happened," I say. "One minute, you were doing fine at Kislev Enterprises, and now you're leaving?"

"I told you—I just need some space." Her shoulders sag. "There are things I love about New York and things I hate. It's time to expand my horizons."

The steward is staring at us. Everyone else has already boarded the flight. I pick up Josie's bag and thrust it into her hand.

"Go. Before I stow away in your carry-on."

Josie flashes me a grin. "Don't worry, I'll be in touch. See ya!"

I return to Vlad's side. He hung back, knowing I'd need a hug when I finally accepted that my best friend was leaving.

When I look back at Josie, it's like she's frozen in time. Her phone is in her hand, and she's staring at the screen as though she's waiting for something. People bustle around her, but she's miles away, locked into a moment of pain that cuts me deep. I take a step, but Vlad touches my arm.

"Sasha," he says.

My camera bag is at my hip. I take it out, flipping off the lens cap, and just as a single tear rolls down her cheek, I take the shot. She pockets her phone and turns away, wiping her face with her palm as she passes through the gate.

Vlad takes my hand. "She'll be okay, *lisichka*."

With Sergey and David dead, the Kislev boys have their work cut out for them. Vlad ought to have been convalescing, but he's been calling meetings with his bratva's associates and renegotiating business terms. It's nothing to do with me, but I wish he'd slow down.

Sasha is now Vlad's second-in-command. He has additional responsibilities, and he's risen to the challenge, but he's not been at the office much. Josie was evasive about her feelings for him, and I guess she hoped he'd turn up at JFK today and beg her to stay.

But life really isn't a movie. Except mine. My life is an action film, a horror, a crime caper, and a romantic epic.

Vlad believed he had to be like his father and that love would destroy him. I thought I was defective, unloveable, and suitable only for horrible men to use. We were wrong and needed one another's love to help us see that.

We barely escaped Cassius with our lives. But he and David showed us what avarice and raw ambition can do when combined with an inferiority complex. They tore themselves apart in vain, trying to seize power and silence the voice inside that told them they were weak.

Of everyone who influenced Vlad as he grew up, his mother won the war for his soul. She made love bloom in the scorched earth of her life, despite all the obstacles in her path.

I wish I could tell her what her sacrifice means to me. Because of her, I have a husband who would destroy anyone at my behest, but I'm not afraid of him. Love gave me the impetus to live, and when I killed Cassius, I murdered the terror that had stalked my mind all these years.

I am *not* defective. I *always* deserved better, and now I have it.

~

When we get home, Lilyana is sitting at the piano, gingerly doing her exercises.

"Aren't you supposed to wear the brace?" I ask.

"I'm trying to do without." She wiggles her fingers. "It hurts less every day, but they get stiff after a while. The physio helps."

Lili's injuries were severe, but she's getting there. Only two of her fingers were broken, and the others were only sprained. She cried for days, terrified she'd never play again, but with careful pain management, she's regaining her range of motion.

"I have something to tell you." She looks from me to Vlad. "Well, I mean, I might have something. I don't know. I'm scared to open it."

"Your letter from Juilliard?" Vlad says. "Are you crazy?"

"No, just terrified." She smiles weakly. "What if I can't play well enough anymore?"

"They know what happened." I take her hand. "Let's just see what it says, okay?"

Sasha is out dealing with business, so Vlad, Arman, Avel, and I sit around the kitchen table. Lili's eyes scan the first few lines of the letter, and we watch her with bated breath.

She chokes back a sob, but then her eyes spill over with tears. She buries her head in her hands.

"Oh, Lili," Avel says. He puts an arm around her shoulder, and she clutches at him.

"I got in!" she cries. "Unconditional acceptance. I can take as long as I need to get back up to standard. Look!" She waves the letter at Vlad. "I did it, Vladi! I'm gonna be a professional pianist!"

I burst into relieved laughter. Arman leaps to his feet and picks Lilyana up by her waist, spinning her around before wrapping her in his arms.

"I'm so happy for you, my *tsvetok*." He kisses Lili's forehead, and her eyes widen in shock.

"Thank you," Lili says. She sinks back into her seat, never taking her eyes off Arman. We all stare at him momentarily, and he sniffs, adjusting his collar.

"What? Good news is good news. I'm just glad it all worked out."

"Yeah." Vlad narrows his eyes at him, then moves on. "That's awesome, Lili. With Avel studying computer science, that's both kids off my hands for a while."

I smile. Vlad acts like the twins are a burden, but it's a family joke. He's more like a parent than a sibling, and he adores them. Stefania would be so proud of him. He'll make a great dad for real when the time comes.

Lilyana hugs me. "I'd never have been brave enough to audition if it weren't for you," she says. "I always felt so helpless. Then you came along and refused to let the past define me."

"That's because of your brother." I smile at Vlad over Lili's shoulder. "He did the same for me. Himself, too."

"I have regrets," Vlad says. "You had more courage than me, Lili. I was more afraid than I realized and had to face it to be worthy of Morgana." He grins. "Am I there yet?"

Lilyana cocks her head. "I think you should keep working at it forever. You know. Just to be sure."

Vlad sits on our balcony, his broad back silhouetted against the sunset. I was gonna get in the shower, but I found myself staring at him instead. How he expects me to get anything done when he's shirtless, I don't know.

"You're a billionaire, and you still wear gray sweatpants?" I ask as he comes inside. "I have to assume you're *trying* to make me drool."

"Ah, yes." He jumps on the spot, pointing at his bouncing cock, and I laugh. "Look at him go. There's no hiding *that*, my love, sweatpants or no sweatpants."

"It wasn't your modesty I fell for," I say, "but maybe don't wander around the house dressed like that?"

He tilts his head, pondering. "I definitely should. It'd establish dominance."

I shake my head. "Sasha would attempt to one-up you by rocking a mankini or something."

He grins, then hisses through his teeth. "Jumping was dumb. I wish this fucking leg would stop bothering me. How am I supposed to pin you to the wall and fuck you if I can't hold you up?"

"We have other ways, Vladi." He lies beside me, and I straddle him, pinning his hands beneath my knees. "I kinda like knowing I could beat you in a fight."

He gawps incredulously as I unbutton my shirt. "*Lisichka*. I will *not* stand for that shit, not for a—"

I bend down, bringing my breast to his lips. He falls silent immediately, to suck my nipple, and I sigh with bliss. I sit upright again, feeling his burgeoning erection stiffening against my sex.

"Do you want to fight me?" I ask. I pinch my nipples between my forefingers and thumbs, and he groans, biting his lip.

"What do you think?" he says. "If I wanted to free my hands, I would. But you're in a mood to torture me, and what can I say? I'm yours to ruin. What my wife wants, my wife gets."

"That's what I like to hear." I kiss him deeply, tasting his tongue. "I'm gonna lose the clothes and lie beside you until I'm ready for you. You think you can resist touching yourself?"

"If that's what you want, yes."

I climb off him and undress, tucking myself under his arm. His fingertips reach for the swell of my breast, and I slap his hand away. "No touching *me* either."

"That's much more difficult," he says. He kisses my neck before wrapping his hand around it, his thumb stroking my jawline. "How about I just do *this*?"

"That's acceptable, but nothing more."

He squeezes just a little as I reach between my legs. My pussy is already heating up, and wetness is gathering in my folds. My fingertip finds my entrance, and I pull some of my lubrication through my pussy lips and onto my clit. The slightest movement of the tiny hood makes me shudder.

"I can't see what you're doing," Vlad whispers hotly in my ear, "but the way your hips are shifting, and your breathing catches... I'm *obsessed*. Let's do this *all* the time."

I enter my needy pussy with two fingers, arching my back as I do so, and his cock lurches in response. It's at full mast now, testing the stitching of his pants. A damp patch darkens the material where the head rubs against it.

"Look at you," I say. "All juicy for me." I rub my clit firmly, bending my knees and pressing the soles of my feet together. "I'll bet your cock needs attention, doesn't it?"

Vlad's grip on my neck tightens. "It *hurts*. Just let me jerk off over you. You don't have to do anything to me but don't leave me like this. I might die."

He sounds wretched, and I almost feel sorry for him, but this is too much fun to let up just yet. "I know," I say. "Be a good boy and wait."

Vlad's words have an edge this time, and I love it. "Don't turn *that* around on me, Morgana. You're my good girl, but I am *not* your good boy and never fucking will be." His fingertips dig into my throat. "And that's how you like it. Isn't it?"

He's right. He lets me take the lead sometimes, but he's the king.

Despite his desperation, he keeps his hands off himself and me. I chase my climax, and he holds me down, the tendons in my neck tight in his grip as he murmurs encouragement.

"Good girl. You gonna make yourself come? I love you. You're doing so well. Look how well you work your hot little cunt."

My fingers are not enough, not with my husband's thick cock there for the taking. "I need you inside me, Vladi. Fuck me, please!"

He releases my neck and rolls me onto my side, facing away from him. He supports my leg, holding it away from my body so he can slide into me, and I groan as he fills me with a single firm thrust.

"Fucking tease," he growls. "I love it, but you're exploiting my weakness." He withdraws entirely before skewering me again, and I gasp. "When I fully recover, you'll get it, Morgana."

His words seem to come from miles away, and I'm only dimly aware of them. I'm consumed by sheer sensation, my fingers working my clit as he surges relentlessly in and out of my clinging pussy. My orgasm is so intense it's almost painful, powering from my clit and sending a shockwave of rapture through my body.

Vladi is right there with me. As my wetness drenches him, he grabs my hips, holding my pussy onto his cock as he pumps his come into me. We lie in that position for a minute before he pulls free, and as I move to sit up, he puts a hand on my stomach.

"Stay there. I'm not letting you wash me away." His fingertips stroke my smooth mound, teasing my sensitive clit, and I sigh. "You lie there while I give you another. I'll spend the rest of my life devoted to pleasing you."

EPILOGUE

Three months later...

Vlad

The villa used to belong to my mother's grandfather. The people of the town care for it all year round, and in return, they help themselves to the lemons and lavender that grow all over the estate.

I can see why she loved it here. The sun-baked brick is homely and comforting, despite the size of the place. The pool is a perfect azure rectangle framed by neat rows of Italian cypress trees.

Morgana runs to her parents, and seeing them throw their arms around her warms my heart. Her mom looks well-rested, the dark circles under her eyes nowhere to be seen. George reaches to shake my hand.

"I love this place," he says. He glances at his wife and daughter as they chatter. "Jasmine has never felt better."

I'm ashamed that I never asked Morgana what her mom's name was. It just didn't come up. "I'm glad. Is she still getting her medication?"

He nods. "Delivered weekly by a little old man on a golf buggy. We don't understand one another, but I'm trying to learn some Italian. He brought us some bread last week too."

The townsfolk are taking care of them. All I want is for them to have the peace they need for Morgana's mom to stay well.

We sit outside, the table piled with grilled fish and crisp-looking salads. Morgana piles her plate.

"So, do you have plans for while you're here?" George asks.

"Absolutely," I say, pouring wine. "We'll take you on a tour of the region. You need to get to know it well if you're staying here permanently."

George and Jasmine exchange looks. Jasmine puts her hand on mine.

"Really?" she asks, her eyes shining.

"Morgana tells me what you say when you call her. How much you love it here, how sad you'll be when you have to come home." I smile. "So I'm saying it—you don't have to. I'll sell your house, tidy up all your affairs. If you want to live here and be the property's permanent caretakers, I'd be grateful. You'd be doing me a big favor."

Morgana claps her hand over her mouth as George stares at me.

"I never imagined you'd turn out to be a good man, Vladi," he says. "Thank you."

"You don't even have to miss Morgana too much," I say. "She can take the jet and see you anytime, and if you want to return to America, you need only say the word."

"We'll look after the place," George says. "It's beautiful. Morgana tells me it was your mother's family home?"

"It was." I lean back in the chair and draw a deep breath, enjoying the smooth sweetness of the lavender. "This is where she grew up. She was happy here."

We eat lunch, and I'm contemplating a dip in the pool when my wife sits beside me, taking my hand.

"Don't get comfortable. We have somewhere to be."

I frown. "And you're taking me there? You don't know this place. Where are we going?"

"It's a surprise." She gets to her feet, pulling me with her. "But you're gonna have to break the habit of a lifetime and let me drive."

◞

After an hour, we turn onto a long dirt track and pull up outside a large house. Although the place is isolated, it's well-kept, with beautiful flower beds and a neatly trimmed lawn. Morgana retrieves a holdall from the trunk of the car, then rings the doorbell. A woman in a nurse's uniform answers it.

"I'm Morgana Kislev. I called a few days ago?"

"Ah yes," the nurse replies in perfect English. "This way, please."

Now that I'm inside, it's clear that the place is a residential home for the elderly. It's a little run-down but has plenty of staff. We pass a lounge where several older people are sitting in easy chairs, watching *Roman Holiday* with subtitles.

"He's in the conservatory," the nurse says, waving us through. "Bring him back to the lounge when you're done, *per favore*."

I'm confused. Mama's extended family no longer live in the area, and most of them emigrated to America anyway. Who are we here to visit?

A man sits in a wheelchair, facing the window, with two chairs set out beside him. "Signore Vertolli?" Morgana says, touching his hand gently. "I'm Morgana. We spoke on the telephone?" She gestures to me. "Here is Vladi."

We sit, and the old man turns his head to look at me. He's in his late seventies and turned out smartly in a shirt and tie, his dark hair slicked back.

"*Mio Dio*, my boy," he says, his eyes filling with tears. "How you look like her!"

"This is Luca," Morgana says. "Stefania's love."

My mouth falls open. I know I must look ridiculous, but I can't help it. My hand flies to my chest, feeling for Mama's ring. I've been wearing it around my neck, keeping her close to my heart.

"I...I didn't know I'd meet you today," I say. I shake his hand. "Forgive me. I don't know what to say."

"It doesn't matter." He smiles at me. "I'm glad to see you. I'm an old man, and I have no family left. No one has visited me in ten years, but don't pity me." He winks. "I'm happy enough. When you get to my age, all you want is ice-cream and a good book."

Morgana unzips the holdall and takes out the bundle of letters. I showed them to her weeks ago, and we spent an evening reading through them.

"Remember these?" She hands them to Luca.

"Of course, *bella*." He smooths the ribbon with his thumb. "Stefania wore this in her hair. She was such a carefree girl. So happy, so kind. It hurts me to find out what happened to her, but I'm glad she is at peace." He closes his eyes. "I never married and I didn't move away. Instead, I stayed, hoping she'd come back to me. She was the only love I had, and I lost her." He sighs and opens his eyes again, looking at me. "And you know something? She was *worth* it."

I reach around my neck and remove the chain, holding it out to Luca.

"Here. Please take this." I place the ring on his palm. "It was hers. She'd want you to have it."

He closes his fingers around it. "I remember this ring. *Her* mother wore it. She wanted so much for her daughter to be happy, and not in a heartless marriage like her own. You'd have loved your Nonna, Vladi. She's the person that gave Stefania the strength to be a good mother to *you*." He tucks the ring into his shirt pocket and pats it. "I will cherish this. You don't know the kindness you do to come all this way and talk to me. I'm honored. It does not surprise me that your Mama raised such a good man, even in terrible circumstances."

"We plan to scatter Stefania's ashes near her home," Morgana tells him, "but we don't know where would be best. Do you have any thoughts?"

Luca takes her hand and kisses it. "As a matter of fact, I do."

~

We drive out to the place the following morning. It's not far from town, and at the early hour, there's no one around.

Morgana helps Luca out of the car, and he walks slowly but steadily over the gravel path. The church is a ruin, left over from Etruscan times, and there are still some ancient gravestones sticking up like loose teeth from the overgrown grass.

Luca points. "Over there. That tree."

We reach the oak, and he places his hand on the trunk, feeling around. "This tree was not so tall when we were here. It may be too high up." His wrinkled fingers move over the bark, and he unpicks a small patch of lichen. "Aha!" he says, pulling the moss away. "Right here."

There's something carved deep into the wood. *LV + SR. Sempre innamorato.*

"Always in love." Luca puts his fingertips to his lips and presses a kiss onto my mother's initials.

Morgana takes a few steps back and pulls out her camera. She doesn't take any time to frame the shot or adjust the lighting, and with a quick motion, she takes the photo.

"I carved this for her," Luca says. "This was our special place, where we could be together without her father's watchful eyes on us. Here, we could just *be*."

My eyes fill with tears. Morgana hands me the urn, and I sprinkle the ashes around the tree.

"*Amore di Dio*, my Stefania," Luca murmurs. "God's love be with you."

Morgana takes his arm and helps him to a wall, sitting beside him.

"What do you do for work, *bella*? Or are you a kept woman?"

"I just sold an article, actually. About Vladi. He'd never given an interview to anyone before, so *The New Yorker* was very keen."

She's too modest. She's sold many articles since then. Her work is causing quite the buzz, and those in the know say she's one to watch for the Pulitzer.

"You don't mind that I took a picture, do you?" she asks Luca. "It was so moving. I didn't want the moment to vanish."

"All moments vanish." Luca pats her knee. "You must be sure to treasure them. Especially with the *bambino*. They grow so fast."

"Baby?" I turn to look at him. "What baby?"

He laughs. "Vladi, my son. Your wife is with child. Look at her beautiful face, so serene, so glowing." He shrugs. "I'm no doctor, but you mark my words. There will be a grandchild for my Stefania soon."

～

We take Luca back to the home, with plans to visit again soon. I hand the manager a check as we leave, and she has to sit down when she sees the amount on it. The entire staff waves us an enthusiastic goodbye as we pull away.

Back at the villa, Morgana's parents have been chased away for the evening to a local trattoria. The owners promised to keep them occupied with Aperol and terrible Italian folk songs until long into the night.

I sit on the love seat, watching the Cypress trees shift in the breeze. Morgana disappeared to the bathroom only five minutes ago, but I'm sure I've been waiting for a decade.

My wife appears on the patio, carrying two glasses of white wine. *Damn*. She wouldn't be drinking if the test were positive.

"You mean I drove all around to find a *farmacia* for no reason?" I ask, taking a glass from her.

She grins at me. "This is grape juice."

My heart feels like it will burst out of my chest. "Are you serious?" I cry. I put the glass down hastily and leap to my feet, swinging her around in my arms.

"Careful, you idiot!" she says, laughing. "Not in my condition!"

"How far along? I mean, when? What do we—"

She puts her finger on my lips. "Hush. All in good time."

We sit side by side, and she puts her head on my shoulder.

"I think I know what names you might have in mind, Vladi," she murmurs. "If so, it's alright by me. Whether we have a Stefania or a Luca, we'll adore them either way."

"Mind how you go. Twins run in the family, remember?" I kiss her forehead. "I love you, *lisichka*."

She winds her fingers around mine. "I love you too."

THE END

ALSO BY CARA BIANCHI

Thanks for reading!

If you enjoyed **Ruined Beauty**, you may also be interested in reading my **East Coast Bratva series**. Read FREE in Kindle Unlimited or buy on Amazon.

Join my mailing list here for exclusive updates about upcoming books in the Angels & Brutes series!

East Coast Bratva

1 - Depraved Royals

2 - Twisted Sinner

3 - Vicious Hearts

MAILING LIST

Join my mailing list and get a free spicy mafia romance novel in return. You'll also be the first to hear the latest Cara news!

Click here to join!

∽

Connect with Me!

Follow me on Amazon here: Follow me

Find me on Instagram - @carabianchiwrites

Find me on TikTok - @carabianchiwrites

RUSSIAN PHRASES

Russian is written phonetically in this book, for ease of reading. Any phrase or word used in the story but *not* listed here will be translated in dialogue on the page.

bozhe moy! - my God!

brat - brother

bratan - 'bro'

da - yes

dyadya - uncle

dobroye utro - good morning

dobryy vecher - good evening

komandir - boss/commander

lisichka - little fox

malchik - boy

mladshiy brat - little brother

moya zhena - my wife

nyet - no

poymi menya? - you understand?

sdavat'sya - surrender

tovarishch - comrade

tsvetok - blossom

RUSSIAN PATRONYMICS

It's customary in Russia to use patronymics derived from the father's given name.

Middle names end with -ovich or -evich. The female patronymics end in -ovna or -evna.

Most surnames end in -ov or -ev. Surnames derived from given male names are common. Female forms of this type of surnames end in -ova or -eva.

For example, male members of the Kislev family are formally known by the same middle name, Sergeyevich, and the surname Kislev. Lilyana's middle name is be Sergeyevna. Morgana's middle name is Georgevna, after her father, and both she and Lilyana go by the female patronymic surname, Kisleva.

Because the Kislevs live in the USA, they don't use their patronymics daily or in all interactions. You'll see them used in the story when a character wants to demonstrate deference or demand respect.

Printed in Great Britain
by Amazon